Hans Werner Kettenbach was born near Cologne. He is the author of several highly acclaimed novels, including *Black Ice*, which was made into a film in 1998. He came to writing late in life, publishing his first book at the age of fifty. Previous jobs he has held include construction worker, court stenographer, football journalist, foreign correspondent in New York and, most recently, newspaper editor. His crime novels have won the Jerry-Cotton Prize and the Deutscher-Krimi Prize; five of them were made into successful films. *Black Ice* is his first novel to be translated into English.

BLACK ICE

Hans Werner Kettenbach

Translated from the German
by Anthea Bell

BITTER LEMON PRESS
LONDON

BITTER LEMON PRESS

First published in the United Kingdom in 2005 by
Bitter Lemon Press, 37 Arundel Gardens, London W11 2LW

www.bitterlemonpress.com

First published in German as *Glatteis* by Bastei Verlag
Gustav H. Lübbe, Bergisch Gladbach, 1982

The publication of this work was supported by a grant from
the Goethe-Institut

A CIP record for this book is available from the British Library

ISBN 1–904738–08–7

Typeset by RefineCatch Limited, Broad Street, Bungay, Suffolk
Printed and bound in Great Britain by
Bookmarque Ltd, Croydon, Surrey

1

People thought it was an accident. Scholten didn't.

It wasn't suicide either. Scholten would have sworn to that. Naturally such a strange death was bound to put ideas into certain heads. And very likely scandal-mongers were now going around saying Frau Wallmann hadn't had an accident at all; she'd killed herself intentionally. Don't let anyone try telling Scholten that. He'd give them a piece of his mind.

What nonsense anyway. Why would Erika Wallmann have killed herself? Because that fellow had a bit on the side? He'd been sleeping around for years, starting the moment he married her. And she'd known it as well as Scholten did. Why would she kill herself because of that, after twenty-five years?

Such a beautiful woman.

To look at her, no one would have thought she was forty-six. The way she walked, with a firm, energetic step, the way she held her head, the way she threw it back when she was displeased, always reminded Scholten of the time when her father offered him the office job. She was fifteen then, but you could already see what a fine woman she'd be.

And now it was all over. Scholten stared at the coffin. As the harmonium player began the *Ave verum*, tears came to his eyes. He covered them with his hand and tried to picture her lying there now in her coffin. But he very quickly gave that up.

She must look dreadful. The fall from the flight of

steps to the steep bank. Broken bones and head injuries, they'd said. From the sharp edges of the rocks on the bank. Then two days lying in the lake. And after that the forensic scientists took their knives to her. They probably opened her up entirely. They'd have to, with a drowned body.

Scholten gagged. Taking out his handkerchief he quietly blew his nose, wiped the corners of his eyes, pressed the fabric over his mouth. He sensed that Rothgerber, sitting beside him, was looking at him. Scholten tried to divert his mind by reading the messages on the ribbons of the wreaths.

To my beloved Erika, a last greeting from her Kurt.

The hypocritical bastard. He'd spent a lot on that wreath, obviously, and the coffin and the whole funeral. The chapel was full of flowers and candles. He'd always been open-handed with Erika's money. And now he had it, all of it, no strings attached. The bastard.

Scholten moved slightly to one side so that he could see him. Wallmann was sitting by himself in the front row. Poor fellow, people would think. No children, no family, nothing.

No. Only Erika's money. And the firm.

Enough to drive you round the bend. Scholten stared at the broad, red neck, the dark-blond, well-cut hair, the massive shoulders in the black coat.

Rothgerber leaned over and tapped his arm. He whispered: "That's a handsome wreath you chose. Excellent." Scholten made a dismissive gesture.

Arsehole. When they were arguing in the office about the message on the wreath Rothgerber had been on Büttgenbach's side. Of course the chief clerk is always right. What was it Büttgenbach had suggested? *In silent remembrance of Frau Erika Wallmann.* What nonsense!

2

But Scholten had got his way. The wreath really was a handsome one. And those not too slow on the uptake could read the real meaning of the inscription: *We will not forget our boss Frau Erika Wallmann. From the office staff of Ferd. Köttgen, Civil Engineering Contractors.* Wallmann for one would get the message.

When the coffin was lowered into the grave Scholten was in the third row. The members of Wallmann's bowling club had pushed their ostentatious way to the front. They and their wives, who were all tarted up, had ranged themselves right behind Wallmann and didn't even let Büttgenbach through. Scholten stood on tiptoe and craned his neck to see, but there was a broad-brimmed black hat in the way.

Scholten bowed his head. He moved his lips as his tears flowed. He said to himself: that's not the end of it, Frau Wallmann. I promise you. You can count on me, Erika.

Wallmann did not meet Scholten's glance as he shook hands. He kept looking fixedly down, his eyes red and damp, his chin quivering although he kept it pressed against his chest. One of his friends from the bowling club was standing beside him holding his arm, as if Wallmann might fall over any moment. Would you believe it? What a farce!

On the way back to the cemetery gate, Scholten found himself walking with a group of the Yugoslavian workmen. They had put on their dark suits and black ties. They walked along in silence beside him for a while.

One of them touched his arm. "Herr Scholten, how can such terrible thing happen? Boss's wife was strong woman, healthy. How can she fall off steps, splash, fall in water? Had been drinking, don't you think, Herr Scholten?"

Scholten stopped and grabbed the Yugoslav by the lapels of his coat. "Say a thing like that again and you'll have me to deal with, understand? And then you can pack your bags and fucking go home, get it? Because you'll be out of a job!"

The Yugoslav said: "Let go." Scholten let go. The man was one of the plasterers, hands like shovels, and a head or more taller than Scholten. He brushed down his lapels and said: "*You* no decide when I'm out of a job."

"We'll see about that," said Scholten. He turned away and walked on. The Yugoslavians fell behind.

At the cemetery gate Scholten looked around. Rosa Thelen was standing there alone, wearing a black coat that was now too tight for her. Scholten said, "You can come with me, Rosie."

She blinked her short-sighted eyes at him in the March sunlight and said: "Thanks, but Herr Büttgenbach is giving me a lift."

"Fine. Your arse will have more room in his car." Scholten got into his own vehicle.

"You brute," said Rosa Thelen. "Can't get a grip on yourself even on a day like this."

Scholten had to wait. The four minibuses were barring the road. The workmen got in, jostling each other, and now and then one of them laughed. They were looking forward to the day off and the beer and cold meats that Wallmann had ordered for them in the bar opposite the works. Scholten muttered: "Wait till it's your own wake. Then you won't be laughing."

He followed the last bus but then turned off on the road to the Forest Café. He was sure Wallmann would rather have sent him off to the bar with the workmen, but in the end he hadn't dared to. He had invited the office staff to the Forest Café. Not just the office staff

4

either. Scholten was sure the whole bowling club would turn up. And the people from the Civil Engineering Inspectorate, of course. He had seen the Government Surveyor at the graveside and three or four of the inspectorate's project managers. And all at the company's expense.

Well, it belonged to the new boss now.

2

A couple of flashy cars were already parked outside the Forest Café when Scholten arrived. He was about to leave his own car beside them, hesitated, then drove into the overflow car park behind the building.

Von der Heydt, one of the project managers from the Civil Engineering Inspectorate, was standing in the doorway of the restaurant bar, holding a schnapps glass. He shook hands with Scholten and asked: "How could a thing like that happen, Herr Scholten? I mean, those steps were checked by the Building Inspection people. Surely they can't be all that dangerous?"

"There's nothing wrong with the steps," said Scholten. "But I don't know the details. You'll have to ask Herr Wallmann." He reached for a tray that a waiter was carrying past and took a glass of schnapps himself. Von der Heydt emptied his own in a hurry, put the empty glass down on the tray and picked up another. Placing a hand on Scholten's arm, he guided him over to the table. "Come along, let's sit down."

Scholten said: "Not here, though. I'm sure this is for Herr Wallmann's friends. I'll sit over there."

"No, no, you're Herr Wallmann's guest today too. Come along, sit down. We're all equal in the face of death."

Von der Heydt made Scholten sit on the chair beside him. He raised his glass. "Let's get this down ourselves first. To help with the shock."

Scholten gulped the schnapps down. Von der Heydt

detained the waiter, who was about to move on with his tray, saying: "Hang on a moment, we'll have another couple of those."

He put the two glasses carefully on the table and lit a cigarette. Then he placed his arm on the back of Scholten's char, leaned towards him and said: "Tell me, Herr Scholten, is it true about Wallmann having it off with the secretary in your firm?"

Scholten looked at his schnapps glass.

"What's the girl's name? There she is, over by the fireplace."

Scholten did not look up. He said, "You probably mean Fräulein Faust."

"That's it. Inge, am I right? Inge Faust. Not a bad-looking girl at all. I guess she's worth a mortal sin or so." Von der Heydt laughed.

"Could be," said Scholten.

"But listen, Herr Scholten, she must be at least twenty years younger than Wallmann, am I right? How old is Wallmann, actually?"

"Forty-eight." Scholten twirled his glass on the table-cloth. "And Fräulein Faust is twenty-five."

"Wow! So does Wallmann think he's up to that kind of thing? I mean, sure, he keeps fit. But wouldn't you say this is rather overdoing it?"

"It's no use asking me. Ask Herr Wallmann."

"So it's true? They really are having it off?"

"I didn't say so. There's always gossip."

Von der Heydt clapped him on the shoulder. "Yes, yes, Herr Scholten, I know. I quite understand you don't want to tell tales on your boss. Don't worry, no one's going to hear about it from me."

Scholten picked up the schnapps and tossed it down his throat. Von der Heydt instantly followed his example. Then he looked around. "They're slow with the beer." He wiped his mouth and leaned towards Scholten again. "But you know, Herr Scholten, if it *is* true, people might get ideas. About poor Frau Wallmann, I mean."

Scholten sat very upright and looked at von der Heydt. "What are you implying?"

Von der Heydt went "Ssh" and nodded at the doorway. Wallmann had come in with his friend from the bowling club who had been supporting him at the graveside, the Government Surveyor on his other side and the rest of them behind him. Wallmann invited the Government Surveyor to sit down. Seeing Scholten directly opposite, he frowned. Scholten was about to rise to his feet, but von der Heydt laid a hand on his shoulder and said: "Excuse me, Herr Wallmann, we sat down here just this minute, but is there a seating plan?"

Wallmann said: "No, no. By all means stay put."

One of the tarted-up women took the chair on Scholten's left. Scholten half rose and adjusted it for her. She smiled at him, a sad little smile as befitted the occasion, but her expression was very friendly. Scholten rose again, bowed and said: "May I introduce myself? Jupp Scholten."

"How nice to meet you, Herr Scholten," she said. "I'm Frau Sauerborn."

Scholten said, "Pleased to meet you too," and sat down. He smoothed the tablecloth, pushed his schnapps glass slightly to one side, drew it towards him again.

The woman wasn't bad looking. Dolled up a bit too much in her black costume, but there was real flesh and blood under it. Scholten smelled her perfume and unobtrusively took a deep breath. Pretending to be looking at the door, he let his eyes dwell briefly on her throat. She was no older than her mid-thirties. Sauerborn, Sauerborn. Wasn't that the bowling club member who owned the brewery?

She settled on her chair. Scholten cast a quick glance down and got a glimpse of her rounded knee encased in black nylon.

He started, as if caught in some guilty act, when she said, "Do you work in Herr Wallmann's company?"

"Herr Wallmann's company? Oh, yes. Yes, I work there."

"I mean, I suppose it *is* Herr Wallmann's company now?" She glanced briefly at Wallmann, who was talking to the Government Surveyor, and moved a little closer to Scholten. "Or wasn't it all left to him?"

"Yes, yes, of course it was." Scholten felt this was awkward. Wallmann was sitting too close for comfort. But the woman's perfume won the day. Scholten smiled, moved his mouth closer to his neighbour's ear and said: "There's no one else to inherit."

"That's what I mean." She sat upright, pushed her plate back and forth a little. Then she smiled at Scholten. "Have you worked for the company long?"

"Oh yes!"

"How long?"

"Good heavens. I'd have to think." Scholten acted as if he was indeed thinking. He nodded. "Yes, you could call it a long time." He looked at her. "Thirty-one years."

"That's amazing! Well, now you must tell me how old you are."

Scholten rested one arm on the back of his chair and smiled. "Guess."

She looked at him, put two fingers to her cheek, then shook her head. "It's really hard to say."

Scholten kept smiling. "I'm fifty-eight."

"I don't believe it! No one would think so to look at you."

The waitress leaned over Scholten's shoulder, serving turtle soup. Scholten said: "Could we have a beer too?"

"Coming, sir."

Between two spoonfuls of soup, Frau Sauerborn said: "And what do you do in the firm?"

"Oh, just about everything." He glanced across the table. Wallmann was drinking his soup and nodding as his friend from the bowling club talked to him. Scholten said, "Bookkeeping. Looking after the filing room, that's very important in a firm like ours. Business with the bank. Instructions to the workmen. Organizing the trucks. And checking up on the building sites. You have to keep an eye on everything."

"Just like in our own business. Then you must have been with the company already when Herr Wallmann started there?"

"Yes, indeed. I'd been in old Köttgen's office for four years before Herr Wallmann joined us."

"And he began in the office too?"

Scholten picked up his napkin and dabbed his lips. He spoke into the napkin. "No, you've been misinformed there. Herr Wallmann drove an excavator."

"You don't say! And didn't old Köttgen mind when he married his daughter?"

Scholten laughed and dabbed his lips again. "Old Köttgen – ah, well, you should have known him."

The beer came, and then the main course. Fillet Steak Special, served on toast. After the first mouthful, Frau Sauerborn lowered her fork and leaned towards Scholten. She spoke from slightly behind his back. "Is it true that Frau Wallmann was pregnant – Erika Köttgen, I mean – when she married Wallmann?"

Scholten, his mouth full, nodded heavily. He leaned back and picked up his napkin. "A miscarriage. After the wedding. She couldn't have any more children after that."

Frau Sauerborn nodded and cut a piece off her fillet steak. She was about to lean towards Scholten again when the bowling club member sitting opposite on Wallmann's left pointed his fork at her. "Ria, you noticed the time, didn't you? When did Kurt leave us on Saturday afternoon?"

"It was exactly four-thirty," said Frau Sauerborn.

"And how long does it take to reach your weekend retreat?"

Wallmann shrugged. "Just under an hour and a half. An hour and a quarter if there's not too much traffic on the road to the lake."

The Government Surveyor nodded. "But then it would have been too late anyway. I mean, it wouldn't have been any use even if you *had* arrived earlier."

Wallmann shook his head in silence.

Von der Heydt, knife and fork poised in mid-air, leaned forward and said: "Forgive me, Herr Wallmann, I didn't quite catch that. So the police really did check your alibi, or shouldn't I call it that?"

The bowling club member took a forkful of mushrooms and said: "You can certainly call it that. It was harassment, no less. They questioned us at the bowling club, they even went to see my wife, isn't that right, Ria?"

Frau Sauerborn nodded. "They wanted to know exactly how long Herr Wallmann spent at our place."

"And they even got Büttgenbach to go to the police station," said Herr Sauerborn.

The Government Surveyor shook his head. "Outrageous, if you ask me. Imagine them coming along after such a tragic accident and suspecting someone of murder!"

Sauerborn gestured vigorously, chewed and swallowed. He took a large gulp of beer and said: "They have to. It's the rules. If someone's fished out of the water they have no option but to investigate."

Frau Sauerborn looked at the Government Surveyor. "They can't be sure there may not be something in it."

Wallmann, who had been brooding gloomily, said suddenly: "But there wasn't."

"Exactly," said Sauerborn. "There wasn't. The alibi was absolutely watertight."

Von der Heydt, head still thrust forward, shifted in his chair. "But how could you prove that? I mean, sometimes proof is difficult. Who expects a thing like this to happen?"

Sauerborn propped his elbows on the table. "Well, listen." He began checking points off on his fingers. "Herr Wallmann came back from his sailing trip on Friday evening. He saw to the boat and went up to his weekend house. Then he realized he'd forgotten the files."

Scholten abruptly clutched his ear and then acted as if he were just scratching it.

"What files?" asked von der Heydt.

Wallmann, red-rimmed eyes fixed on the beer glass he was slowly pushing back and forth, said: "Files I needed for a tender I was putting in. I wanted to get the details finalized at the weekend. I thought I'd brought the files from town with me. While I was out on the boat I hadn't realized they were missing."

"You see?" Sauerborn said, nodding. "He didn't notice he'd left the files in town till he got back to the house. But by then his wife was already on her way. She

12

was going to spend the weekend with him out by the lake. So he couldn't phone and ask her to bring the files with her."

"Yes, I see," said the Government Surveyor. "What a tragic chain of circumstances."

"Yes," said von der Heydt, "but I don't understand what that has to do with the alibi business – I mean, what does it prove? To the police, I mean?"

"Just a moment." Sauerborn raised both hands. "I hadn't finished. So he drove off to fetch the files. Just under three hours to get there and back, no problem. And then he saw Erika's car up by the lake, in the village. She'd arrived already. There's a bar with a butcher's shop attached in the village, you see, and when she went to the lake she always stopped off there to buy meat for the weekend. And to drink a little glass of grog. That's right, Kurt?"

Wallmann nodded.

"Grog was her favourite," said Frau Sauerborn.

Scholten crossed his arms over his chest.

"So then what?" asked von der Heydt avidly.

"Well, pay attention," said Sauerborn, "because here comes the alibi." He paused for the waiter to take the plates away and pointed to the empty beer glasses. "Bring us a couple more, will you?"

"And some spirits," said Wallmann. "Not the schnapps you were serving before."

"Cognac, sir?" asked the waiter.

"Yes, cognac," said Wallmann.

Sauerborn settled comfortably in his chair, leaned his elbows on the table, pointed his forefinger at von der Heydt and said: "He went into the bar and told his wife what had happened. And then he set off for town from there, at ten to seven. The butcher, sorry, I mean the barkeep, he confirmed it. Erika was sitting there drinking her grog at the time. And he reached us in the bowling club at eight exactly."

"You must have driven pretty fast," said von der Heydt, "if it usually takes an hour and a half."

Sauerborn laughed. "He's never needed that long. Speedy Kurt, we call him in the club. He always drives that way, don't you, Kurt?"

Wallmann said: "And they call you Randy Günther."

Sauerborn laughed. "So they do."

Frau Sauerborn shifted in her chair and said: "But what's that got to do with Kurt's alibi?"

"Now, now, take it easy," said Sauerborn. "I was only joking!"

Von der Heydt raised his beer glass, noticed that it was empty, put it down again and said to Wallmann: "Hang on a minute, I don't quite understand. So you went to the bowling club before you fetched the files?"

Wallmann nodded. "On impulse."

Sauerborn took a deep breath and let it out again. Then he said: "So there you are. We were living it up a bit that evening. It was our fault."

Wallmann said: "No, mine. I'll never forgive myself."

"Nonsense, Kurt. It could have happened to anyone. And you'd have been back too late in any case. So we got rather merry, and by the end of the evening he wasn't fit to drive. I took him home with me. Better safe than sorry – I know Kurt. And he didn't leave our place until four-thirty on Saturday afternoon. Fetched those files from the office and drove back to the lake. He arrived at the house there just after six."

Von der Heydt leaned back in his chair. "Yes, now I see. So he has what amounts to a twenty-four-hour alibi."

Wallmann was playing with a beer mat. "Just a little over twenty-three hours," he said.

14

"Well, put it however you like, but it was during that time your wife fell off the steps and into the lake."

"On the Friday evening," said Wallmann.

Sauerborn said: "She didn't go into the house at all. Her car was still outside the door, with the meat she'd bought in it and her weekend things."

"You don't say." Von der Heydt rubbed his chin. "So why did she go down the steps? I mean, they lead to the landing stage, if I've understood the situation correctly. Does anyone know what she did that for?"

The Government Surveyor said: "Herr von der Heydt, I think that's enough in the way of questions. This is a wake, you know."

Wallmann put the beer mat down and clasped his hands on the table-top. "I don't know why she did it. I'd give a lot to know. But I really have no idea."

Scholten folded his napkin and then unfolded it. The waitress served ice cream. After her second spoonful Frau Sauerborn said: "It's really odd, her going down those steps. Particularly as she didn't like boats or going sailing, did she, Kurt?"

"No, she didn't." Wallmann pushed his ice away, picked up his empty cognac glass and signalled to the waiter.

"Oh, Ria, really!" Sauerborn's voice had risen slightly. "Sometimes you talk pure nonsense! What's so odd about it? She probably heard a noise and went to see if there was anyone prowling around the boat. After all, it's valuable. Four bunks, heating, toilet. Built-in kitchen. Right, Kurt? Must have cost you a packet, after all."

Von der Heydt's spoon remained in mid-air. "How much, then?"

The Government Surveyor noisily cleared his throat and then asked: "Are you having any trouble with the

Buildings Inspectorate, Herr Wallmann? Over that flight of steps, I mean? Because if I can help you in any way . . . ?"

"No, the steps are fine. Solid timber, with handrails. And made of good stout planks. You only have to ask Scholten here. He replaced half a dozen steps last autumn because they'd developed some cracks. When was it exactly, Scholten? When you went over to paint the fence?"

Scholten felt Frau Sauerborn looking at him. He said: "Yes, it'll have been around then."

The bastard. Wallmann was just trying to belittle him in company. As if anyone would be interested in the fact that he'd painted the fence. Scholten finished his cognac.

The waiter came and refilled the glasses. "Coffee will be served in a minute."

Wallmann said, "Where's your wife, Scholten? I didn't see her at the cemetery."

Scholten swallowed. "She couldn't come. She's feeling unwell again. She asked me to give you her regards and say how very sorry she is."

"Thank you. My regards to her, and I hope she'll soon be better."

Frau Sauerborn asked, "What's the matter with her?"

Scholten shook his head. "Poor health in general. It's her nerves. A funeral like this upsets her too much."

"It upsets us all," said Sauerborn.

Silence fell. After a while von der Heydt said: "Perhaps the steps were slippery? After a frost, maybe? We had that sort of weather last week. Or was it different up by the lake?"

"No, you're right," said Sauerborn. "The steps must have been slippery. Timber like that can get very icy in frost. She wasn't expecting it, she slipped, and she couldn't catch hold of anything to stop herself falling."

The Government Surveyor nodded. "That's perfectly possible. Yes, very likely."

Wallmann rose to his feet. "Would you excuse me a moment?" He went out.

Sauerborn pushed his own chair back. "You must excuse me too. It's the beer."

3

That morning Scholten had planned to leave the funeral party early and go to the brothel on the way home. It was a good opportunity. He could leave the wake on the pretext of Hilde's poor health, and Hilde wouldn't be able to work out when he ought to be home.

But in the end it was almost three in the afternoon when he left the restaurant bar. One of the bowling club members had already stumbled over a chair leg and brought a tablecloth down with him as he fell; two others had taken him out and loaded him into his wife's car. Before that Rosa Thelen had been overcome by a fit of weeping, and Herr Büttgenbach was still sitting in the tearoom with her, trying to comfort her. And von der Heydt, who had moved from his seat beside Scholten after coffee and gone to sit next to Fräulein Faust, had exchanged words with Wallmann and gone off uttering threats. By now the Government Surveyor was dozing off in his chair.

Scholten ate two peppermints when he got into his car. He put the hollow of his hand in front of his mouth, breathed into it and sniffed. Not too bad, he thought.

He joined the motorway. The forest was left behind, there were factories to right and left, suburban gardens, apartment buildings. Blue-grey clouds covered the March sky. It wasn't as sunny as last week, but not as cold either.

Scholten thought of the woman he planned to pick. He had definite ideas about her. He'd find someone with black stockings. Black stockings look terrible on thin legs, but on a nice plump pair, who can resist them? Scholten smiled. He'd never yet seen a girl with thin legs in the knocking-shop.

He tried to paint a clear mental picture of his imagined girl, as he always did on the way to the brothel. But this time he didn't succeed. Scraps of the conversation around the table at the wake kept getting in the way.

The alibi, oh yes. Herr Wallmann had thought it all out very neatly. And what about those files? He'd forgotten about them, or else he'd thought Scholten was so stupid he'd never notice. The hell with that.

So he has no idea why Erika was going down to the boat? What a laugh! He knows perfectly well what Erika was looking for on that boat. So does his bit of fluff Fräulein Faust. You bet your bottom dollar she does.

Then that fool van der Heydt comes out with some tale about slippery steps. And of course Sauerborn takes the bait at once, positively falling over himself to provide an alibi. A watertight alibi. He had to be joking! Maybe Sauerborn's actually in cahoots with Wallmann.

Slippery steps after a frost. Rubbish.

Scholten rubbed his eyes. He felt there was something missing from his chain of thought. Something didn't fit. He shook his head, took his hand off the steering wheel, muttered to himself: "Just a moment! No point trying to think now, Jupp Scholten. You've had too much to drink. Let's go and have it off with a girl, and then take a good nap. And hope to heaven Hilde doesn't make a scene again. Then we'll sit down and think about it at leisure. It'll be an odd thing if we can't work out what that fellow was up to."

He still had to pass two more motorway junctions before reaching the exit road that would take him to the brothel when his foot suddenly slipped off the accelerator. The car swerved slightly before Scholten was back in control and concentrating on his driving. He swore, looked in the rear mirror, got into the right lane. Here came the next exit. He took it. He looked at the time. "Hell. All the Wops will be there at four."

He hesitated a moment at the traffic lights. If he rejoined the urban motorway now he could be at the brothel before it had its rush hour.

However, he turned off to the city centre instead and looked for a phone box. He looked up the number of the local paper in the phone book and dialled it.

"Daily News, how can I help you?"

"My name's Scholten. I'd like to speak to the person responsible for the weather."

"Responsible for the weather?"

"Well, not like that – I mean whoever writes the weather page in the paper. The weather forecasts."

"I'll put you through to Miscellaneous."

"Just a moment, miss, I only want . . ." He listened. Nothing. She'd broken the connection. "How stupid." He looked out at the traffic, and a nasty idea occurred to him. It had been a mistake to give his name. You never knew. Better to give a false name. As he was still thinking, a man's voice came on the line.

"Frings here."

"Er, good afternoon, this is – this is Höffner speaking."

"Good afternoon, Herr Höffner."

"I'd like some information, please. I always read your paper. I take it every day."

"Yes? So what can I do for you?"

"I wanted to ask if you can tell me whether there was a frost last week. In this region."

"A frost?"

"Yes, if it froze. Slippery roads and so on, understand? Last Friday. In this region. Did you get that?"

"Yes, of course, but I can't tell you off the cuff."

"Why not? I was told you're responsible for the weather reports."

"Yes, I am."

"Well then, you must know. I mean, there can't have been a frost, can there? We had bright sun all week. On Friday too. Even on Saturday."

"Just a moment, Herr Höffner. That was the name, wasn't it – Höffner?"

"Yes."

"Let's make sure we understand each other, Herr Höffner. You want to know whether the roads can be slippery with frost in weather conditions such as we had last week, is that correct?"

"Yes, exactly. Particularly on Friday evening."

"Okay, okay. I'll make some enquiries."

"What do you mean, make some enquiries? Don't you know?"

"Herr Höffner, I'm not a meteorologist. I'm a reporter, understand?"

"Yes, yes, I understand."

"I'll ask the Meteorological Office for you, Herr Höffner."

"How long will that take?"

"You want to know today?"

"Yes, of course I do."

"Okay. Call me back in half an hour."

"Can't it be any sooner? I have some other urgent business. I'm in a phone box."

"Okay, let's say fifteen minutes. Till then, Herr Höffner."

"Wait a minute! What was your name again?"

"Frings, Herr Höffner."

"Yes, yes, fine."

Scholten hung up and looked at the time. Damn it, the brothel would be bursting at the seams. And Hilde would kick up a fuss. She was never going to believe the wake had gone on this long.

He left the phone box and walked up and down. He tried imagining the girl in black stockings. They usually wore boots with them. He stared at the pavement, but the picture refused to take shape. That reporter had got him all muddled up. What was the man's name again? Frings. What a useless idiot! Had to call the Met Office for the answer to such a simple question.

But the Met Office wasn't a bad idea. They'd come up with cut-and-dried evidence. Frosty roads in bright sunshine. Total nonsense. They were probably laughing themselves sick at the Met Office.

Suddenly he saw the woman clearly in his mind's eye. She wore black stockings and black boots. Her basque was tightly laced, everything spilling out above it. Scholten slowly walked on, looking at the ground. He went as far as the corner, stopped. He stood there for some time. Suddenly he looked at his watch. He swore, hurried back to the phone box. An old woman was just reaching out for the door handle. He opened the door and pushed past the old lady. "Just a moment, I was here first."

Someone had been turning the pages of the phone book. Scholten cursed, found the number of the newspaper. Through the glass, he could indistinctly hear the old woman's voice.

"Daily News, how can I help you?"

"This is Höffner, I'd like to speak to Herr Scholten. No, I mean Herr Frings. Herr Frings!"

"Which Herr Frings? We have two of them."

"The one on the weather page. The one who does the weather forecasts for you."

"I'll put you through."

Scholten did not turn round. He could still hear the old lady's voice.

"Frings."

"Höffner here. I'm calling back about the weather."

"Yes, Herr Höffner, here we are. Right, listen: in weather such as we had last week – high pressure, no cloud, sunny by day but very cold by night – in weather like that there can easily be frost. Particularly close to water. The atmospheric humidity sinks by night, you see. In temperatures above zero it forms dew, and if the temperature drops below zero it forms frost instead. Is that clear, Herr Höffner?"

"Are you telling me that's what the Met Office said?"

"Oh, come on, Herr Höffner. I feel this conversation is getting a little difficult. I told you I called the Met Office in Essen especially on your behalf."

"Yes, yes, all right. Thanks." Scholten hung up and said: "Bastard."

He pushed past the old lady, who was standing close to the door of the phone box as if she intended to bar his way. Raising her voice, the old lady said, "What rudeness, what impertinence! You ought to be ashamed of yourself, you ought!"

"Go boil your head," said Scholten.

He got into his car and sat there indecisively. He looked at the time. "Oh, hell, oh, bloody hell!" But still he did not drive off. He rubbed his forehead.

Frost on the roads.

He didn't believe it.

Perhaps this Frings hadn't called the Met Office at all. Too much bother for him. He only said he had. He simply made it up. Scholten had got on his nerves, so he'd done it to pay him out.

Scholten hit the dashboard with his fist. "I'll stop taking that paper! They're not going to fool around with me!" He leaned over to the glove compartment and fished a peppermint out of the roll. It tasted horrible. He wound the window down and spat the peppermint out into the road. A beer would be good now.

He still didn't start the car. He stared through the windscreen. It began to dawn on him that von der Heydt's idea hadn't been so bad. And probably the police had thought of it too by now.

Frost on the steps.

Erika had driven up to their weekend house from the village. That was around seven. The sun had already set. Erika had gone down the steps at once. He knew why, and Wallmann knew why, and Wallmann's bit of fluff knew why too.

Perhaps she hadn't even switched on the light at the top of the steps, so as not to be seen too soon. And then she'd slipped and failed to catch hold of the handrail, found nothing to break her fall, and plunged from the steps to the steep bank and from the steep bank into the lake. Broken bones, head injuries. She was probably unconscious by the time she went into the water.

Scholten cursed. He started the engine and drove away. He rejoined the urban motorway and left it again at the next exit.

There were not as many cars outside the brothel as he'd feared. He hurried into the contact area where you viewed the girls, slowed his pace, looked around.

24

A girl approached him and took his arm. "Hi, darling! How about it, then?" She was wearing red boots and flesh-coloured tights.

Scholten smiled and shook off her hand, went on.

One of the girls sitting on a sofa in the dim, reddish light said, "Leave the man in peace. He's just buried his old lady, he's still in mourning."

The women laughed. Scholten smiled.

He went on again, rather faster. In the final corner before the exit he found what he was looking for. Even the basque was right, tightly laced. A foreigner was standing beside her, black hair, black moustache, a small, stocky man in pullover and jacket. She was talking to him.

Scholten stopped three paces behind the couple. He half turned, pretended to be inspecting the other women again. He straightened his tie, cleared his throat. It felt tight. He looked at the couple again. The foreigner took a step towards the exit. The girl held him back by his arm. The foreigner smiled.

Scholten stepped up to the woman and tapped her on the shoulder. "How much?"

The foreigner took a step forward and looked at Scholten. "You get out."

Scholten said: "What's the matter with you? I can stand here as long as I like."

The foreigner said: "When I speak to woman, you no business here. You get out."

"Hey, what's with the pair of you?" said the woman. "Let's cool it here. Well, what about it, Mustafa? Coming?"

"I not Mustafa."

"Makes no difference. How about it?"

"Him get out first."

Scholten said: "Him not want to."

"You not know nothing. When I with woman go, it not your business."

The woman looked at Scholten. "Can't you wait ten minutes? I'll be back in ten minutes."

Scholten cleared his throat and said: "Now or never."

She looked at him. "Trying to make trouble? Push off, Grandpa."

The foreigner gestured with his thumb. "You hear that? Push off, Grandpa."

Scholten left. When he was out of the contact area he said: "Lousy bastard. Stupid cow." A large old car was standing beside his: battered, covered with dust, brightly coloured cushions on the back seat. Scholten looked around and then kicked the door hard with the toe of his shoe. "Garlic-eater."

4

Scholten couldn't find anywhere to park outside the front door of his building. He had to go three buildings further on. Before getting out of the car he cupped his hand in front of his mouth again, breathed into it, sniffed. He wondered whether to eat another peppermint. No, ridiculous. They didn't help anyway.

When he had got out of the car he stood there for a moment. He took a deep breath. The air was cooler again; it did him good. The many little windowpanes of the long, three-storey apartment buildings reflected a rosy glow. The sun was low in the sky. It cast its reddish light on the windows, the curtains, the pot plants standing on the windowsills. The rooms behind the windows lay in twilight.

Scholten looked in his letterbox. It was empty. He climbed the stairs. There was a smell of pickled beans on the first floor again. Old Mrs Kannegiesser must be preserving tons of them. And you could buy the stuff for a few pfennigs in the supermarket.

He suddenly stopped on the second-floor landing. He rubbed his forehead. His hand froze. He looked at the floor, then up again when he heard a sound behind one of the front doors of the two apartments on that storey. He climbed a few steps further, far enough not to be seen through the peepholes in the doors. He stopped again, hand on the banisters, eyes lowered, thinking hard.

That nonsense about suicide. He'd been sure from

the first that it couldn't be right. What a slander! And now he had something like evidence that she hadn't jumped off the steps, she'd fallen.

Slippery frosty steps. But could Wallmann plan that in advance?

And can you slip on frosty steps anyway? It's possible, yes. But she wasn't an old woman, she wasn't unsteady on her legs. If there'd been actual black ice, yes, that could make the steps really dangerous. But not frost. Of course, if someone had pushed her . . . And he had thought of that too, he'd thought Wallmann had lured her out on the steps and pushed her down.

But it was impossible. That damned alibi. Wallmann would never have been in town as early as eight if he'd driven back up to the house and pushed Erika off the steps first. It simply couldn't be done. Scholten narrowed his eyes as a new idea came to him. Perhaps the members of the bowling club were lying? Perhaps Wallmann hadn't arrived until after eight, maybe half an hour later? That would have been time enough.

Scholten shook his head. Surely not a whole bowling club. And the landlord and the waitress. And in a case like this too. You couldn't get a bowling club to do it. He knew that from the days when he used to go bowling himself. You couldn't even drop into the brothel without someone telling tales afterwards.

No, it wouldn't have worked.

Yet there was something wrong about the alibi. He knew there was.

The files. Exactly. Wallmann had looked in at the office on the Monday before driving out of town to take the boat out of its winter quarters and set off on his sailing trip. He'd come into the office, done some phoning, and then he said Scholten was to deal with the mail and look out the files for the tender, he wanted to take them with him. Fräulein Faust wasn't there. She'd taken a week's holiday. To go and see her friend, apparently. For a baby's christening. What a laugh.

He had found the files for Wallmann and put them in a folder on his desk. And when Wallmann had gone, the files had gone too. And Wallmann couldn't have put them on one side by mistake and forgotten about them, because they were nowhere around the place.

As always when Wallmann and Fräulein Faust were not there, Scholten had poked around Wallmann's office a bit. But he hadn't seen those files. He'd have noticed them.

There was only one explanation: Wallmann had locked the files in his desk before leaving. No one was to find them. He didn't want Erika bringing them with her on Friday.

Why?

To give him a reason to drive back into town on Friday evening.

Or perhaps he had taken the files with him, but even then he was lying, because he claimed to have fetched them from his office on Saturday.

Maybe it really was a watertight alibi. But if so, then Wallmann had prepared it carefully in advance.

Why would he do that?

Scholten whispered: "You bastard, you bloody bastard. How am I going to find out your tricks?" He stared at the wall of the stairwell, which was painted yellow. When he heard a sound above him he jumped.

Hilde said: "Joseph? What are you doing out there on the stairs?"

He said: "Just coming up."

She stood there on the landing, one hand on the

banisters, holding her cardigan together with the other. He went past her into the apartment.

She closed the door. "You're not going to tell me the funeral lasted all this time, are you?"

He took off his coat and jacket, hung them up on the coat-rack, removed his tie. "What do you mean, funeral? I told you there was going to be lunch at the Forest Café afterwards."

"It must have been a very good lunch. I can smell it from here."

"It *was* a very good lunch. Turtle soup, fillet steak, an iced dessert. You could have gone too."

"You know perfectly well I couldn't."

Scholten went into the bathroom. Behind him, she said: "Dr Küppers told you about my blood pressure."

He stood in front of the lavatory. He heard her say: "It won't flush properly again."

His urine made a loud noise splashing into the bowl. Scholten broke wind.

"You might close the door!" she complained. "So vulgar!"

He kicked the door shut behind him. When he'd finished he took the lid off the cistern. The ballcock was stuck again. The hell with these cooperative apartments! He'd told the caretaker twice already that they needed a new ballcock. He let the cistern fill up, then flushed. The ballcock worked this time.

When he came out of the bathroom she was standing in the kitchen doorway. She followed him into the bedroom. He took off his shoes, put shoetrees in them. He put on his slippers.

She stood there at the door, hand still clutching her cardigan. "Surely you're not keeping your good trousers on?" He took his slippers off again and opened the wardrobe.

She said: "You can put your old blue trousers on. I don't suppose you're going out again, are you?"

He put on his old blue trousers and his slippers, hung the black suit up on its hanger and put it in the wardrobe.

She watched him. She said: "So that lunch is supposed to have lasted all this time?"

"My God, I had to talk to the guests! The Government Surveyor was there, and some of the project managers from the Civil Engineering Inspectorate. And other customers of ours too. That man from the Cooperative House-building Association, the ringleader – you know how they all stick like burrs."

The cat rubbed round his legs. He bent down to tickle it. It began purring. "Has the cat been fed?" he asked.

"Of course, what do you think? Are you suggesting I'd let the poor creature go hungry?"

"I don't know what time you got up. You told me you had to rest in bed."

He went into the kitchen. Hilde followed him. He took a bottle of beer out of the fridge.

"Haven't you had enough of that?" she said.

"Oh, good Lord." He looked at the ceiling. "Can't a man even drink a beer?" He went over to the kitchen table, took the bottle opener out of the drawer. "I'm sure I don't know what else life has to offer."

She said, her voice sounding a little thinner: "I got up at twelve. And I didn't go back to bed after that."

"Why not?" He raised the bottle to his lips.

"Because I was worried about you." She began to weep.

Oh, for God's sake, this was all he needed. He almost swallowed the wrong way, wiped his mouth. "All right, all right. Come on, stop crying." He went over to her, patted her on the back. He couldn't bear to see her face, so miserably distorted, it was a pitiful sight, there was no bearing it. "Come on, stop crying. I'm sorry. But I really couldn't get away."

She took a handkerchief out of her cardigan pocket, wiped her eyes, blew her nose loudly.

He patted her on the back again. "I did think you might be worrying. I'm sorry."

Her voice still miserably thin, she said: "You shouldn't drink out of the bottle. Why not get a glass? It tastes much better from a glass."

"Yes, yes, I'll get myself a glass. Look, you go and lie down again now. Can I bring you anything?"

"No, I just want to lie down. I'll get up and make supper at six."

"Yes, fine."

"Would you like fish fillets?"

"Yes, yes, very nice."

He watched her walk away. In the doorway she turned. "Would you rather have fried potatoes or boiled potatoes?"

"Fried potatoes. I could really fancy fried potatoes."

"I have some potatoes left over from yesterday. And a lettuce. Will that do?"

"Yes, of course it will do."

"Then I'll go and lie down now," she said.

"Yes, you do that."

The bedroom door closed.

Scholten went back to the kitchen table and raised the beer bottle to his lips. Yet again he almost swallowed the wrong way. He went to the kitchen cupboard, fetched a glass and poured some beer into it. He drank the rest from the bottle.

5

Scholten had finished his drawing just after five-thirty. He had fetched a pencil, an eraser, a ruler and a few sheets of paper from the living room. Out in the hall he stood still, listening. No sound from the bedroom. He had taken another bottle of beer out of the fridge, carefully and quietly closing the door.

When he went out on the balcony to put the empty bottle back in the crate and take two full bottles out, the cat had followed him, mewing. "Yes, all right, I know – you want to go for a walk."

He had put the cat in its basket and lowered the basket to the garden with the reel of cord he had mounted on the balcony rail two years ago. He tied the cord in place and watched the cat. It jumped out of the basket and disappeared into the bushes.

He quietly closed the door to the balcony, put the two full beer bottles in the fridge and sat down at the kitchen table.

He looked at his drawing. He had been up and down those steps a hundred times, most recently last autumn when he was taking the cooker and the bottled gas and the heater out of Wallmann's boat for the winter. But it was odd how few details lingered in his memory. He had had to think hard about the number of steps, and he still wasn't entirely sure.

Anyway, first there were five steps leading straight down from the open space behind the garage. Then came the landing, three planks side by side on the same level. The joints didn't fit very tightly. Then the steps turned at a right angle and went on down, twelve or thirteen of them, maybe even fourteen, adjoining the left-hand side of the landing and going down to the lake.

Getting the correct perspective for the right angle had given Scholten some trouble, but the result was not bad. The steps had been built like that in order to bypass the steep slope of the bank. You could see the slope in Scholten's drawing, and the little sandy bay to which the steps led, and the landing stage on its floats projecting out into the lake from the bay.

You could also see where the bank came up to the steps on the left-hand side of the sandy bay, and on the right-hand side you could see the narrow path along the bank where he had once walked with Erika. They had strolled through the wood and come down to that path. And then they had followed the path to the bay and climbed up the steep bank to the house again by way of the steps.

Scholten studied every detail of his drawing and suddenly nodded. If Erika had really slipped on the flight of steps it could only have been on the landing, where they turned at an angle, or on one of the treads just above it. If it had happened lower down, beneath the landing, she would probably have fallen into the sand of the bay. But if she had slipped on the landing or the steps above it, she could perhaps have fallen right off the landing to come down on the steep bank and then fall from there into the lake.

Was that really possible?

The landing was a good twenty-eight inches deep. She could surely have found something to hold on to. Perhaps not the handrails at this point, but one of the vertical posts supporting the steps and the handrails. Frost, yes, all right. But does someone so steady on her feet just fall flat if she happens to slip?

Scholten raised the beer bottle to his lips.

Hilde said: "Why are you drinking out of the bottle again, Joseph? You've got a perfectly good glass in front of you!" She was standing in the kitchen doorway.

Scholten slammed the bottle down. "Good heavens, what a fright you gave me! Why do you always creep around like that?"

"I'm not creeping around. The cat's mewing down in the garden. It wants to come up again. Didn't you hear it?"

"No, I didn't." He stood up. The cat was indeed mewing.

She came over. "What are you doing?"

He gathered the sheets of paper together. "It's for a construction drawing." He wanted to take the sheets with him but didn't dare; he left them lying on the kitchen table. He went out on the balcony.

The cat was already sitting in its basket, looking up and mewing. "Yes, all right, come on up." He hauled the basket up and over the balcony rail. The cat let him lift it out; he stroked it, and it immediately began to purr. When he wound the cord up it put its head on one side, reached out a paw and patted the cord. "Now then, stop that. We'll be needing it again. Go and find your ball."

When he returned to the kitchen Hilde was standing by the table looking at the sheets of paper. "What does it show?"

"Those are the steps outside Wallmann's weekend house."

"What are you drawing them for?"

"I'll have to go out there again some time. There's probably another couple of planks need replacing."

"When are you going to stop doing all this extra stuff? You're not Herr Wallmann's odd-job man!"

"Oh, for goodness' sake! He pays me well for it. We can do with the money."

She went to the fridge and took the fish fillets out of the freezer compartment. She said: "I think you just do it to be alone. And so you can leave me on my own here."

"Bloody hell! Are we starting in on that again?" He put his drawing things together. The pencil fell on the floor.

Raising her voice, she said: "You shouldn't swear!"

"Yes, okay. What's so bad about it if I go up there now and then? It's a beautiful place. Fresh air. The woods. It does me good."

"Why don't you ever take me?" she said.

He carried the drawing things into the living room.

When they were sitting at the kitchen table, eating supper, she said: "Will you write to the children after supper?"

"Maybe. I'll see. Could be I'll do it tomorrow."

"Helmut's letter came two weeks ago. And Angelika's has been lying around for nine days. I'm sure they're expecting a reply."

"Oh, come on, you don't believe that yourself. That was the first letter from Angelika in three months. And it was even longer since Helmut last wrote."

"That's not true. Helmut wrote after Christmas. At least they want to know how we are."

"Yes, sure."

"I'd do it myself if it wasn't such a strain on me."

"Yes, yes, I'll do it tomorrow." He wiped his mouth and went into the living room. Out in the passage he belched discreetly. He switched on the TV set and sat down in the armchair. During the news he fell asleep.

He jumped when Hilde touched his shoulder. "There's no point sitting in front of the TV and then falling asleep," she said. "You might as well save the power."

He rubbed his hands over his face. He felt very thirsty.

She pointed to the TV set. "Well, there's your Federal Chancellor for you."

"He's not just my Federal Chancellor, he's yours too."

"I didn't vote for him." She wrapped the rug round her legs and lay down on the sofa.

"Yes, I know. You vote for the capitalists. Like Herr Wallmann."

"Well, at least Herr Wallmann has made something of himself."

"You could put it that way." He rose, went into the kitchen and took a bottle of beer out of the fridge. He looked for the glass. Hilde had washed it up along with the plates and cutlery and put it back in the cupboard. When he came back into the living room he said, "The fish was rather salty." She gave the beer bottle a glance of silent reproof.

He fell asleep twice more in his armchair. When Hilde had nudged him for the second time he got to his feet. "I'm going to bed."

The cat was already in its basket. It blinked at him when he switched on the bedside lamp, rolled over and stretched its legs. He tickled it a bit. "There we are. Now then, time for bye-byes."

Hilde came in as he was getting undressed. She turned away from him. She sat down on her own bed before taking off her vest over her head. He saw her pale, thin back. She reached for her nightdress, put it on as she sat there. She lay down, smoothed out her quilt with both hands, then tucked it firmly round her on both sides. When he had switched off the light she put out a hand, touched him on the shoulder and said: "Good night." He replied: "Good night."

He waited and then heard the faint whispering sound. She was saying her prayers.

A little light from the street fell into the room on both sides of the curtain drawn over the window. A car drove past.

Scholten listened. He heard footsteps on the stairs. Someone passed their door and climbed up to the top-floor apartment. It must be the boyfriend. One of the boyfriends. He had seen at least three different men climb the stairs since the woman on the top floor moved in. But the cooperative wasn't interested in that kind of thing. They were just keen to rake in the cash.

The ballcock. He would call the caretaker on Monday. Honrath the caretaker was bone-idle, that was his trouble. You had to light a fire under his arse. What else was he going to do on Monday? There was something else he'd meant to remember.

Scholten fell asleep.

6

He woke with a start, not knowing where he was, when Hilde patted his quilt. "Has that cat got into bed with you again?" she asked.

"The cat? What do you mean?" He rubbed his eyes, groped for the bedside light. He felt the cat on his feet. It was just curling up.

"I heard it, I'm sure. Take a look."

He switched the light on. Hilde was lying flat on her back, the quilt up to her chin. She had raised her head and was looking at the bottom of his bed. "Put it in the basket," she said. "You must get it out of that habit. It's not healthy. That cat moults."

Scholten got out of bed, picked up the cat. "There now, Manny, back you go in your basket." The cat purred loudly. He put it in the basket and tickled it under the chin a little. When he turned away the cat raised its head and looked at him. He wagged his finger. "You stay there like a good boy, or there'll be trouble."

He got back into bed. "Bloody animal!"

"You shouldn't swear!"

"No, all right." He switched the light out.

He lay on his side. After a few minutes he turned over on his back. He stared into the darkness. He was wide awake. It took him some time, but in the end he could make out the shape of the wardrobe. A faint reflection of light from the street lamp outside was shining in the mirror fitted to the middle door.

Scholten saw the chest of drawers too. The big mirror on top of it was in the dark, but its outlines too emerged more and more clearly.

It takes you some time to see things in the dark.

Perhaps Erika hadn't even switched on the light at the top of the steps. And then there was the frost. But if she'd simply slipped in the dark – then was it an accident after all? And Wallmann's alibi fitted that scenario. He couldn't possibly have pushed her off the steps.

But then why had Wallmann set that alibi up? You surely can't foresee an accident?

"Hold on a moment," Scholten told himself. "This is no good, Jupp Scholten. You're going round in circles. With something like this you have to begin at the beginning and go through it all in the proper order."

He settled himself in bed, pulled up the quilt, pushed the pillow under his head. He listened for a moment. He could hear the faint, regular sound of Hilde's breathing.

Very well. Wallmann drove out of town on Monday last week. And Fräulein Faust didn't come into the office at all. She was taking a week off for the christening. She said she was going to see her friend in Passau and stay till the weekend. Just the same time as Wallmann was allegedly going to be away on his own.

"I'm going to take the boat out of its winter quarters, then I'll spend a few days sailing on the lake. I need to relax and be on my own for once," he had said. And that fool Büttgenbach had nodded earnestly, as if agreeing that Wallmann worked too hard and needed a rest.

Erika had known exactly what to think of this sailing trip. On Thursday, when she came into the office, she had asked Scholten: "Has my husband called?"

"No, not yet."

"Didn't he say he was going to?"

"Yes, he said he'd ring the office now and then, to find out what was going on."

"Oh well, he's probably very busy." She had sat down at Wallmann's desk and looked through the papers Scholten had found for her.

Scholten had watched her for a while and then said: "Hasn't he called you either, then?"

"Me? What makes you think he'd call me?" She went on vigorously leafing through the papers. "He wouldn't do that. I might ask questions."

Suddenly she had raised the papers in the air and slammed them back down on the desk. "That sh. . . that boat! It ought to be burned! Do you know what that thing cost, Herr Scholten? Twenty-four thousand nine hundred marks, and that's before the extras he had fitted. A 'nifty little cruiser'! Oh yes. I'd like to see that nifty little cruiser go up in flames. It stinks. Do you know what it stinks of, Herr Scholten?"

Scholten had picked the papers up again. She'd said: "Pour me a schnapps, Herr Scholten. And one for yourself too. Come on, let's drink a toast. To life. And human beings. Aren't human beings just wonderful?"

She had tossed the schnapps down her throat and held her glass out to him. As he refilled it she had said: "But not for very much longer. I've just about reached the end of my tether. And then there'll be no more sailing, believe you me, Herr Scholten. Then he'll be in for a shock. And the nifty little cruiser will be sold, because I was the one who paid for it. Or perhaps I really will have it burned. That'd be quite something, don't you think, Herr Scholten? A bonfire in celebration!"

He had shaken his head. "I wouldn't do that. You'd

get a lot of money for it. The boat's in really good shape." Scholten raised his feet under the quilt. He was getting hot. He tried another position, pushed the quilt a little way back, rearranged the pillow under his head. He listened for a moment. He couldn't hear Hilde's breathing. But then it came again, that faint, regular sound.

Scholten scratched his belly. That had been Thursday. And then on Friday he suddenly called at three in the afternoon. As if there was any point in that when the week was practically over. Scholten was in Wallmann's office; Erika was sitting at the desk when the phone rang. Scholten picked it up and heard Wallmann's voice.

Wallmann asks if anything particular has happened, and Scholten says no. But his wife's here, says Scholten, does he want to speak to her? Erika takes the receiver, and Scholten turns to go, but she gestures to him to stay.

Then she says, "What do you mean? Of course I'm coming over. I've packed my things already. I think I can leave in a couple of hours' time . . . yes, around five. But I'll stop off at Grandmontagne's for some meat. I should think I'll be with you at the house around seven. Why ask? . . . Oh, I see. And it could take some time? . . . Very well. Where are you now, anyway? . . . Ah. Right. Anything else? . . . No, not here either. Right, see you soon."

She hangs up and looks at Scholten. "Do you know what a mainsheet is, Herr Scholten?"

"Mainsheet?"

"Yes, or something like that."

"It's the rope you use to work the mainsail. What about it?"

"He says he has a problem with the mainsheet. He's

taken the boat into the yachting basin to get it seen to. He doesn't know just when he'll be at the house."

"The mainsheet? What's wrong with it?"

She suddenly stands up. "How long will it take him to get from the yachting basin to the house?"

"That depends on the wind. He won't use the engine. A good hour, maybe two. I'm not sure."

She reaches for her bag in haste and puts on her coat. She points to the desk. "Never mind all that stuff. I don't need it any more."

"Yes, but – are you going to start now?"

Slowly, she comes back, sits down at the desk in her coat, puts her bag down. She looks at the desk for a long time. Then she says: "You're right. It won't be any good. He's too crafty." She looks at him. "But if I knew for certain, Herr Scholten, if I knew that I could catch him, then I would. And one of these days I will too. I've been looking forward to that moment for a long time."

"Would you like a schnapps?"

"Yes, come on, Herr Scholten, let's have a schnapps. Perhaps it will cheer us up."

She rises and takes her coat off again.

They sat there for another two hours, talking of this and that. Of the old days. The sun had faded, the blue sky outside the window had turned a little darker. Just before five the phone rang again. She picked up the receiver, gave her name, said "Hello?" and "Hello?" again, and then she hung up.

"Who was it?"

"I don't know. Didn't answer."

They had both, he was sure, been thinking the same thing: it was Wallmann. He wanted to find out if she was still in town. Why?

She had put her coat on, picked up her bag, and left. Scholten had seen her to her car. He had taken her keys to open the car door for her. She had waved to him as she drove away. And that was the last time he ever saw her.

Scholten felt the tears come into his eyes. You bastard! He gritted his teeth. A small strained sound escaped him: half pain, half fury.

He jumped in alarm, raised his head slightly from the pillow and listened. Yes, he could hear Hilde's breathing. He let his head fall back and relaxed.

It was perfectly clear, and now he could see it all in the right order of events.

Wallmann had left the office on Monday morning. He had picked up Fräulein Faust and driven to the house with her. And then he got her to drive him to the yachting basin. No, wait, that would have been too risky. He had probably called the village to order a taxi to drive him to the yachting basin. He had got his boat out of winter quarters.

He had gone back to the house in the boat and taken his bit of fluff on board. And then they'd gone for a sailing trip. Yes, it must have been very comfortable. The big double bunk in the foreship. Heating. They could cook on board too. And the lake was a good size, no one could find them in a hurry. Not that there were many people out on the water at this time of year, in the middle of the week.

He probably planned to be back quite early on the Friday so that he could drive his bit of fluff back to town before Erika arrived. Maybe even on Thursday evening. No, that would have been one night less for them. Naturally they'd want to have fun up to the last minute.

But then he had problems with the mainsheet. He went into the yachting basin. His bit of fluff probably stayed in hiding below decks. He had called the office

44

at three to find out when Erika was driving up. And whether he had enough time to get his bit of fluff away.

Erika had seen that at once. That was why she wanted to leave immediately, at three. She wanted to catch the pair of them arriving with the boat. But then she had second thoughts; she didn't think it would work. "He's too crafty." Of course. He could put his bit of fluff ashore somewhere in the yachting basin, and she could have caught the bus home.

But he didn't do that. Obviously a real gentleman like Wallmann doesn't let his bit of fluff go home by bus. He had the mainsheet repaired, and then they went to the weekend house. And he called again from there, around five, and hung up again at once. He just wanted to find out if Erika was still in town and if he had time to get out of there with his bit of fluff.

Hold on a moment, Jupp Scholten. Something doesn't quite fit.

Wallmann had still been in the village at a quarter to seven. He looked in at Grandmontagne's while Erika was sitting there with her glass of grog and said he had to go back to town for the files. If he'd still been at the house at five he would have set off with his bit of fluff at once. He wouldn't have hung about until quarter to seven.

Scholten thought hard. Suddenly he drew a deep breath.

Of course: Wallmann was still in the yachting basin at five. The repair had taken some time. He was in the yachting basin when he called the second time. And hung up. They could still get back to the house. Then he put the bit of fluff in his car, looked in at Grandmontagne's and said he had to go back to town for the files, and he drove his bit of fluff back.

No. No, Jupp Scholten, that doesn't work either.

Even Wallmann wouldn't have the nerve to drive past Grandmontagne's, right in the middle of the village, with Fräulein Faust in his car.

And there was another thing: if they'd come back in the boat so late, he couldn't risk driving along the track through the woods to the road with his bit of fluff in the car. Erika might have met him on the way. The track is too narrow for cars to pass each other. You have to give way. She'd have stopped, asked where he was going. She'd have seen Fräulein Faust.

No, he must have been alone when he drove away from the house. Fräulein Faust can't have been in his car. But where was she then, where was his bit of fluff?

Still on the boat, maybe?

Scholten sat up abruptly. In alarm, he glanced at Hilde. She didn't move. He cautiously sank back again and smoothed the quilt.

He smiled grimly in the darkness. Yes. He knew what had happened now for certain. He'd worked it out. He'd found the answer.

Where was Wallmann's bit of fluff? Simple. She was still on the boat. Or no, not on the boat. She was up at the house. Behind the garage. In hiding.

Wallmann had fixed it all so that Erika would be bound to think his bit of fluff was still on the boat. That call at three in the afternoon and his question: was she coming up for the weekend as they'd arranged? And then the problem with the mainsheet. Very likely he'd damaged it somehow himself, to give him an excuse to be seen at the yachting basin. The repair was probably done by the time he called at three. But he wanted Erika to think he had problems, so that he'd be back early enough to get his bit of fluff away unnoticed.

Hence the call at five. He also wanted to make sure

46

that Erika wasn't already on her way. But at that time he wasn't in the yachting basin any more, he was back at the house with Fräulein Inge Faust on his lap. They were sitting there waiting, and shortly after six-thirty he drove off, looked in at Grandmontagne's and made out he was in a great hurry. And Erika fell for it and thought he was in a hurry because he had to get his bit of fluff away. Along the path by the shore, for instance. Of course: Erika thought he was planning to get his bit of fluff out along the path by the shore.

So she drove up to the house and immediately climbed down the steps.

Or planned to climb down the steps. But Wallmann's bit of fluff was behind her. She came out of hiding and pushed her. And Erika fell from the steps, hit the steep slope of the bank, and from there she fell into the lake.

That was it. That was how it must have happened.

And Wallmann had his alibi.

Scholten smiled grimly. Well, he needn't think he was getting away with it.

He cautiously sat up, smoothed his pillow flat and lay down again. He massaged his belly. He stared into the dark. Something was still worrying him.

Wallmann's bit of fluff. What about her own alibi? It wasn't in good shape.

Really? Wasn't it? She'd been telling everyone she was off to Passau to stay with her girlfriend. And the police had probably been too stupid to check. Why should they? They probably didn't even guess that Inge Faust and Wallmann were an item.

And how would Inge have got back to town? Wallmann was already on his way. He had his alibi to think of.

Scholten rubbed his forehead. Then he smiled to

himself. How silly. It was perfectly simple. She got back to town the way she came to the house. In her own car.

She had hidden her car in the wood before they set off on their sailing trip. No, wait. That would have been too risky, leaving it for five days. And why bother? They had simply put her car in the garage with Wall-mann's. And when they came back with the boat on Friday afternoon they had taken her car out and hidden it behind a bush somewhere. Then, after pushing Erika down the steps, Wallmann's bit of fluff got in it and drove home.

Scholten took another deep breath. He settled in bed and smoothed the quilt out. He closed his eyes. He smacked his lips with satisfaction.

After a while he felt his penis stiffening. He opened his eyes and listened. Slowly, he drew his knees up and cautiously unbuttoned his pyjama trousers.

Hilde said: "You needn't think I'm asleep. I can hear everything you're doing. You ought to be ashamed of yourself. Stop it at once."

Scholten turned on his side and pulled the quilt up over his shoulders.

After a few minutes he fell asleep.

7

On Saturday Scholten thought hard about what to say on the phone. He mustn't make it too long. The police record such conversations. He didn't know how well he could disguise his voice, and if he went on at length someone might recognize it on the tape. "Hey, that's Scholten, Superintendent. He's disguised his voice, but I swear that's him."

When he went downstairs to fetch the newspaper from the letterbox he was muttering to himself: "Check Fräulein Faust's alibi. Inge Faust, she's a secretary with Ferdinand Köttgen, Civil Engineering Contractors. The owner of the firm, Frau Wallmann, didn't die by accident, she was murdered. Check Fräulein Faust's alibi."

He was pleased with the idea of making the first and last sentences identical. You had to show the police where to begin, and the repetition would make sure they got the point. If not, they were just useless. But the whole thing was much too long. They had ways of tracing your call, and before he'd finished they'd know where he was calling from.

Hell, that was true anyway. He stood motionless on the stairs with the newspaper in his hand. He couldn't call from home. Or from the office. He'd have to use a phone box.

That was dangerous. He'd been thinking of putting his handkerchief over the receiver to distort his voice. But he couldn't do that in a phone box: too much risk of someone seeing him.

"Shit," said Scholten.

The woman from the top floor was coming downstairs. She said: "Good morning." Scholten stepped aside, smiled and said: "Good morning. How are you today?"

"Fine, thanks. How about you?"

"Ah, well – as good as an old man feels when he sees a pretty young woman."

"Oh, go on with you!" She laughed. "You're not telling me you're an old man, are you?"

He stepped up to the banisters and watched her on her way down. "That depends."

She looked back, laughed and waved to him.

What bodywork, he thought, good breasts too. He climbed the stairs in his slippers.

"Who were you talking to out there?" asked Hilde. She had opened the front door of the apartment just a crack.

He went in past her. "Frau Lewandowski."

"What did you have to talk to her about all that time?"

"Good heavens, she just said good morning, and I asked how she was."

"You could have spared yourself that question. Bad people always feel fine. Anyway, it's not *Frau* Lewandowski. She isn't even married."

"You want me to say Fräulein Lewandowski to her?"

"I don't know why you have to say anything to her at all. You know perfectly well there are always men going in and out of her place."

"Yes, yes."

"But I suppose that doesn't bother you. Maybe you'd like to go up to her place yourself?"

Scholten retreated to the lavatory with his newspaper.

50

He put the paper down on the edge of the bathtub, propped both forearms on his knees and thought. He silently moved his lips. After a while he had found wording that satisfied him. "Frau Erika Wallmann of Köttgen Civil Engineering didn't die in an accident. She was murdered. Check Inge Faust's alibi." That contained the essentials but wasn't too long. He could be through with it in six or seven seconds.

He could leave out the "Frau" too. If necessary even the name of the firm. Instead he might repeat "Inge Faust's alibi" at the end. Ten seconds, he didn't need any more to get the message across. Then out of the phone box and off as fast as he could go. There was just the problem with the handkerchief. He couldn't risk that. Maybe he could whisper? What he was saying must sound distinct, of course.

Hilde called through the door: "What are you doing in there? Talking to yourself? Don't stay on the lavatory so long. It's not healthy."

He found no chance all day to get to a phone box. It was obvious he'd have to drive to another part of town. He couldn't call from the phone boxes near his own apartment. Too many people knew him and might ask: "What was he doing in a phone box? Surely he has a phone at home!"

When he picked up the shopping bag to go to the supermarket Hilde said she would come too. She was feeling better, she told him.

Oh, he said, but he wanted to look in at the works again. Wallmann wouldn't be thinking about the maintenance of the trucks only a day after the funeral, and Rothgerber and Kurowski never did it properly. He was going to the works to make sure the men were cleaning the trucks properly, or they'd arrive at the building sites filthy on Monday morning.

51

Hilde said he'd do no such thing. Why were Herr Rothgerber and Herr Kurowski project managers, drawing a higher salary than he did? She didn't see why he should do their work for them. Or Herr Wallmann had better make him a project manager too.

Scholten gave up. He felt a certain relief. He hadn't really thought it all through properly yet. Whispering might not be safe enough.

At Mass on Sunday morning he had an inspiration. His thoughts had been going round and round in his head, and when the organ finished the prelude *Beim letzten Abendmahle* he missed the vocal entry. Hilde nudged him, and Scholten joined in, . . . *die Nacht vor seinem Tod*, with the powerful tenor voice of which he was still rather proud.

As he sang loudly, clearly giving the note for the people in the pews around him, he could almost have smiled. Of course, that was how he could do it: he could say his piece in a head-voice. Then no one would recognize him easily on a police tape. No one at all, that was certain. They might even take him for a woman.

But on Monday morning, on the way to the works, he drove past all the phone boxes. Sometimes he couldn't see anywhere to park; sometimes he reached a set of lights just as they changed to green.

At six-thirty he turned out of the street into the works' yard. His car rattled over the deep ruts that the builders' trucks always left in the trodden mud. The sky was cloudy; it had begun to drizzle. Two windows of the low office building were lighted. The sun, pale and veiled, was just rising above the ridge of the wooded land to the east.

Scholten wiped his shoes on the scraper outside the door and went in. The soft manmade flooring laid over the wooden boards muted his footsteps. He looked in at the filing room. Rosa Thelen stood there, holding a coffee cup.

"What are you doing here so early, Rosie?"

She drank her coffee. "I couldn't sleep."

"You ought to go dancing in the evening. Then you'd sleep all right."

"Oh, do be quiet."

"Believe me, I know what I'm talking about." He went to his locker, hung up his coat and jacket, put on his grey overall.

Rothgerber appeared in the doorway of the project managers' office. He was holding the duty notes with the day's assignments for the truck drivers. "Morning! Here, you could give these out. And tell Wielpütz to drive exactly where it says on that note, none of his side trips."

"Yes, yes, calm down. There's no one here yet." Scholten took the note and went to join Rosa Thelen in the filing room. "Do you have a cup of coffee to spare for me, Rosie?"

He sipped the coffee, winked at her. He sang: "Rosie, Rosie, give me your answer, do . . ."

"Oh, don't go on like that."

"Why not? You know I think you're fun."

"Yes, I know. First you act all friendly, and then you turn mean. Like on Friday. And at a funeral too."

"What did I say on Friday?"

"Don't pretend you've forgotten."

"Oh, that." He drank more coffee. "But that was a compliment, you know it was." He lowered his voice a little. "Rosie, how often do I have to tell you your arse makes me randy?"

He put out his hand, trying to get hold of it. She

struck his fingers away. Scholten laughed. He put the cup on his desk and went out.

Kurowski, out of breath, met him in the doorway. "Lord, what traffic again."

"You ought to start a little earlier, Herr Kurowski. Then you'd miss the traffic."

"I'm not as daft as you." Kurowski opened his locker.

"Dear me, young people today." Scholten went outside the door. The yard was gradually filling up. Three or four dozen men were standing around. They had put their yellow jackets on and were talking, smoking and yawning.

Scholten found the truck drivers and gave out the duty notes. Wielpütz looked at his and pushed his cap to the back of his head. "What's all this, then? Who filled this note in? That Rothgerber?"

"Never mind who filled it in. You're to drive exactly the route it says on the note, no side trips."

"Fuck him." Wielpütz threw his cigarette end away.

"You want to go carefully, my friend." Scholten pointed to one of the trucks. "Is that yours? Number Four?"

"Yup, why?"

"Never heard of care and maintenance of your vehicle?"

"Fuck you too."

Scholten glared at Wielpütz. Wielpütz returned the glare. Scholten said "Like I said, go carefully, mate," and moved away.

Rothgerber came out of the hut and discussed the day's programme with the foremen. The diesel engines of the minibuses and trucks started. Blue vapour from the exhausts drifted through the yard.

Scholten liked the knocking of the engines, their deep growl, the acrid smell of the exhaust gases. He

54

stood on the scraper outside the door of the office building, put his hands in his overall pockets and watched them leave. He was a little cold in spite of the pullover he was wearing under his overall. It would be warm inside the offices by now. Rosa was probably pouring fresh coffee. He wondered whether he could take another of the black cigars from the box kept for visitors without Wallmann noticing.

At seven-thirty Scholten was sitting at the little desk in the filing room, opposite Rosa Thelen, drinking coffee, smoking a black cigar and reading the paper. He gave the paper back to Rosa when he heard a car door slam outside, but it was only Büttgenbach.

Scholten set to work on the filing. Fräulein Faust wasn't in yet. No doubt that would become a habit now. Scholten looked out of the window. Surely Wallmann wouldn't have the nerve to take her to bed in his apartment already? But he was capable of anything. In Erika's house. In Erika's bed. And Erika herself only just underground.

Scholten pushed the folder he was holding violently back into its place.

Rosa Thelen looked up. "What's the matter?"

He puffed at his cigar, put it down on the ashtray. "Oh, Rosie, you simple country girl."

"Are you starting on that again?"

"No, no, it's all right, calm down." He took another file out of the cabinet, opened it and went to the window. Wallmann needn't think he could get away with this. He was reckoning without Jupp Scholten.

He'd call the police on the way home this evening. Evening would be better anyway. He could turn off into a side street and look for a phone box and a parking place at his leisure. There were phone boxes well hidden away down side streets.

He looked out of the window and moved his lips soundlessly.

"Keep a watch on Herr Wallmann's house." No, this was getting much too long. What was it he'd intended to say again? "Frau Erika Wallmann didn't die in an accident, she was murdered. Check Inge Faust's alibi." Not quite as long as he'd thought. Maybe he could add, "Keep a watch on Herr Wallmann's house."

Inge Faust's little car came through the gates. It swerved alarmingly and stopped outside the office building. She got out, leaned into the car and came back into view with a stack of mail under her arm. Scholten watched her balancing on one leg and kicking the car door shut with the other. Her handbag impeded her. She tried to hold the stack of mail down with her chin, approaching the door and taking small steps. He heard her struggling with the handle. The door flew open. Inge Faust cried: "Herr Scholten, Herr Scholten, quick!"

He went out and took the stack of mail from her. She heaved a small sigh – "Oof!" – and smiled at him. "I dropped in at the post office – now no one has to go out for it." He carried the stack of mail into her office and put it on the desk.

"But they won't have had it all ready at this time of day."

"Oh, most of it's just junk mail." She took her coat off. "I thought you'd be glad if I brought it with me."

"Yes, of course." Standing beside the desk, Scholten spread the mail out with his hand, as if by chance.

She opened the coat cupboard, looked in the mirror, took her headscarf off and shook out her short curls. Scholten looked at her. As she put her coat in the cupboard he examined her back and then cast a brief sideways glance at the mail.

He saw the blue envelope at once. It had been franked at the yachting basin's boatyard and bore the place's logo, a red and blue pennant in a circle.

She had taken out her comb, looked in the mirror again and ran it through her hair. She adjusted the scarf at her throat.

"Shall I open the mail for you?" asked Scholten.

"Oh, no thanks. I'll start on it straight away. But you could get me some water. I really need a coffee. Would you be kind enough?"

Scholten took the jug out of the coffee machine. "How much water?"

"Enough for four cups please."

He went to the washroom, taking his time about it. When he came back she was busy opening and sorting the post.

"Where do you keep the coffee?" asked Scholten.

"Oh, you're so kind! Down there to your right in the little cupboard. The key's in it."

Scholten took coffee and a filter paper out. "Four cups, you said?"

She laughed. "Herr Scholten, whatever has come over you today? Well, yes, four cups if you don't mind. I'm sure Herr Wallmann will be here soon too."

Scholten elaborately unfolded the filter paper. "Level spoonfuls?"

"Slightly rounded, please."

As he poured the water in she stood up. "There, that's done."

He inspected the filter, put the coffee in, said, as if casually: "Shall I take the mail?"

"No, I'll do it. I don't want to disturb your coffee-making."

She picked up the larger stack of mail, smiled at Scholten and went into the project managers' office.

Scholten immediately strode over to the desk, pushed two letters aside and pulled the blue sheet a little way out. It was an invoice from the boatyard, very short. *To replacing one tackle (mainsheet)*. The price of the tackle followed. And the price for labour: half an hour.

Scholten pushed the blue sheet back and arranged the other two letters on top of it again. He went into the filing room, very nearly forgetting to switch the coffee machine on.

The cigar had grown cold. He lit it again, puffed at it, triumphantly watched the blue clouds rise. Rosa fanned the smoke away with her hand.

He'd known it. The bloody bastard!

Even if he'd only just reached the yachting basin when he called at three, he could have set off again half an hour later. They'd simply taken out the tackle and put a new one in. And the hypocritical bastard acted as if he didn't know how long he'd have to hang around or when he could be back at the house.

It was perfectly clear. Erika was supposed to think he was having difficulty in getting his bit of fluff away in time. And that was exactly what she did think.

Inge Faust was standing in the doorway, cup in hand. "You must make me a coffee more often, Herr Scholten. This is really good!"

When she had gone again Rosa said: "Well, fancy that. You never think of making coffee for me."

"Rosie, your own coffee is unbeatable. She doesn't know how to make a good coffee, does she?"

"She may know how to do other things."

"So do you. Or even if you don't, I can teach you. You only have to say the word."

"Oh, do give over."

Wallmann arrived at eight. He went into the project managers' office, looked in on Büttgenbach in his little room then disappeared into his own office. He passed the filing room without going in.

A little later Inge Faust appeared, saying: "Herr Scholten, would you please come into Herr Wallmann's office for a moment?"

8

Only as he entered Wallmann's office did Scholten realize that he still had the stub of the cigar in his mouth. He reached for it as if lost in thought and let his hand drop to his side, turning it in to hide the cigar stub. Wallmann, gulping coffee, followed the progress of the stub with his eyes. Inge Faust stood bending over the side table, sorting papers.

"Yes, Herr Wallmann?" said Scholten. Wallmann slowly emptied his cup. He looked at Scholten over it. His eyes were still red-rimmed. He put the cup down. "Scholten, were you at the Jagdweg building site on Thursday?"

"Thursday?" Scholten felt hot under the collar. "Yes, I was."

"What were you doing there?"

"I was asked to take Hülsenbusch that note from Herr Kurowski. Saying there was something wrong with the drawing."

"Yes, you were asked to. But you didn't."

Scholten swallowed and then said: "What makes you think that?"

"Don't answer back." Wallmann leaned both forearms on the desk. His head was slightly lowered, and his red-rimmed eyes looked up at Scholten from beneath his brows.

He looked quite threatening. "You went from here to the Cooperative House-building Association excavations and collected the stuff for Rothgerber. Then you met Wielpütz and simply gave him the note for the Jagdweg site. And Wielpütz, the lazy bastard, forgot about the note and left it in his vehicle."

Scholten wondered frantically what he could say.

"You know what we'll have to do now, Herr Scholten? We're going to have to take out the Jagdweg pavement and put it back again properly. I've just been to the site, looking at the mess they made of it."

Scholten shook his head, expelled air through his lips. "Can I help it if Wielpütz forgot the note?"

"I don't think you understand me. This is not about Wielpütz, I'll be talking to him too. This is about you. If you're told to drive to the Jagdweg then you drive to the Jagdweg, by the quickest route there is. You can't be so stupid that you didn't know it mattered. You probably went into a bar for a quick drink. When were you back here?"

"I can't remember now. I'm going all over the place the whole time." Scholten cleared his throat. "And you have no right to call me stupid."

"Scholten, I think you still don't get the idea. Next time I shall make a deduction from your salary. You're getting too expensive. This is not a charity organization. Oh yes, and something else occurs to me. Would you give me the cigar box, Fräulein Faust?"

Inge Faust handed him the cigar box from the occasional table. She went out.

Wallmann lifted the lid of the box, looked inside it. He called: "Fräulein Faust?"

She came back. "Yes?"

He gave her the box. "Please lock the cigars up at once."

Scholten took a deep breath. "Are you suspecting me of stealing?"

"What do you mean, suspecting you? You're the only one here who smokes cigars."

"Oh, come on, Herr Büttgenbach smokes cigars the whole time."

"Going to brazen it out too? Scholten, you really do not get the idea." Wallmann leaned heavily on his forearms and looked at him. "You are definitely becoming too expensive for me, Herr Scholten. Now go back to your work." Without taking his eyes off Scholten, he picked up his empty coffee cup and held it out to Inge Faust.

Scholten turned away. In the doorway he said: "This is outrageous. I don't have to put up with this sort of thing. It's scandalous."

He was going into the filing room but turned and went to the toilet. In the corridor he said: "Shit-head! Bloody bastard! Arsehole!" He sat on the lavatory in his overall and bolted the door.

The bastard wouldn't have dared do that when Erika was alive. But no sooner was she buried than he got going. They were all in for a nasty shock. Kurowski for sure. Büttgenbach too. He couldn't cope with his work any more. He was always getting Scholten to find him stuff that he needed. What was the betting that Büttgenbach really had helped himself from the cigar box now and then?

Talk about a shabby trick!

Oh no, Herr Wallmann, you don't mess about with me. Not with Jupp Scholten. You've picked the wrong man there.

But Scholten felt fear rise in him. It rose from the pit of his stomach up to his throat.

Erika wasn't here any more. Everything belonged to that bastard now. He could do as he liked.

He felt the sweat break out. He put his hands under

his arms, took hold of his pullover through the overall and pulled it back from his armpits. He unbuttoned the overall, took out his handkerchief and mopped his forehead and temples.

He'd call the police this evening. The fellow had made a mistake. He'd get a shock. Someone had to put a stop to his goings-on.

When the coffee break came he was feeling a little better. He went over to the project managers' office. Rosa Thelen had taken Rothgerber his coffee, and Kurowski was out with Wallmann inspecting the building sites.

Rothgerber unpacked his sandwiches. He opened the desk drawer and took a bottle out. "Would you like one?"

Scholten sat down at Kurowski's desk. "I won't say no."

Rothgerber carefully handed him the schnapps, looked at him. "How could you give Wielpütz that note? It was bound to mean trouble."

"Cheers!" Scholten tossed the schnapps back. "Why does he have to get so worked up? He's made mistakes often enough himself."

"Yes, I know, Herr Scholten." Rothgerber chewed, picked a few crumbs up from the paper wrapping his sandwiches. "There's just one little difference: he's the boss now. The boss in person."

"Yes. I'd noticed."

Rothgerber leaned forward. "If you'll allow me . . ." He broke off and looked over his shoulder.

Inge Faust came in. "I've got something to show you all. Just a moment, let's ask Herr Büttgenbach in too." She called: "Herr Büttgenbach! Do come in here, would you?"

Büttgenbach came out of his little room with Rosa

Thelen behind him. Inge Faust opened an envelope, took out a folder of photographs, handed the first one to Büttgenbach.

"Oh, how sweet!"

Rothgerber stuffed the rest of his sandwich into his mouth and stood up. Rosa Thelen looked over Büttgenbach's shoulder.

Scholten pushed back his chair. "What is it?"

"Photos of the christening," said Inge Faust. "When I was on holiday. My friend sent them."

Rothgerber said: "You look good like that, holding a baby." He passed the photo on to Scholten.

"I should hope so!" said Inge Faust. "I was godmother."

Scholten took the photograph. He stared at it. Then he dropped back into his chair.

The photograph showed Inge Faust carrying a baby in a christening robe. She was bending her head down to the child and smiling.

Scholten took the next photograph without looking at it. "When was the baby's christening, then?" he asked.

"A week ago last Friday." Inge Faust sighed. She bit her lower lip and shook her head in silence. Then she said: "Yes. The day Frau Wallmann had her accident."

"Oh, shit," said Rothgerber. "That's life."

9

It took Scholten several hours to get over the shock. He didn't want to admit that his theory had been wrong.

For a while he clung to the idea that Wallmann's bit of fluff was lying. Who was to say her girlfriend really lived in Passau? Maybe she lived in Düsseldorf or even closer. She could easily have left Düsseldorf to drive out to the lake on the Friday afternoon and hidden in the garage.

But then he remembered that in some of the photos the christening party was standing outside a large church, and someone had said it was Passau Cathedral; yes, it was Büttgenbach. Büttgenbach was an idiot, and Scholten didn't believe a word he said. But Inge Faust couldn't hand round photos of such an unusual church and say it was in Passau if it wasn't in Passau at all.

Anyone could have recognized the church. No, Wallmann's bit of fluff wasn't that stupid. Not her.

Ah, but then who was to say that the christening had really been on the Friday? Why not the previous Monday? Or even the Sunday? Christenings are usually on Sundays, right? Then Inge could have driven back on Sunday afternoon or evening, she could easily have met Wallmann at the lakeside house on Monday, and there'd have been nothing to stop the sailing trip. Or the murder.

Scholten clung to this explanation for some time.

He relinquished it only when suddenly, in a fit of rage that afternoon, he found himself inadvertently saying out loud: "And I'll make that phone call this evening, you bet your life!"

Rosa had looked at him in alarm. "Would you like another coffee?" she asked.

"No, no, thanks all the same. Just thinking aloud. One has to do that sometimes, you know."

"Or shall I get you a beer?"

"Yes, a beer, please." He had found the money for the beer and given it to her. "Here, I only have eighty pfennigs in small change, you'll get a groschen back."

While she fetched the beer from the crate in the storeroom he realized that he might wreck everything if he called the police. Because if they checked Fräulein Inge Faust's alibi, and the alibi stood up, Wallmann was out of the woods once and for all. It couldn't have been Fräulein Faust. And it couldn't have been Herr Wallmann either, they'd think, because he had a watertight alibi too. And after that no one would be able to persuade them that it wasn't an accident. Or suicide.

Although it hadn't been an accident, and certainly not suicide.

Scholten raised the bottle to his lips, drank, wiped his mouth, belched. Rosa Thelen looked down at her paperwork.

Erika had been murdered. No matter what they said. Perhaps Wallmann's bit of fluff really had been away all week at that christening. Perhaps she really did have an alibi. And Wallmann had one too, a watertight alibi.

But why had Wallmann set his alibi up? Because he *had* set it up, that was one hundred per cent for sure. So why?

And why had he fixed everything so that Erika would

think he was off sailing with his bit of fluff? Because he'd done that too, also one hundred per cent for sure.

Why go to all that trouble? Why any of it?

In front of the TV that evening, Scholten brooded. Hilde had said she wanted to see that evening's episode of *A Convent in Lower Bavaria*. She was lying on the sofa, a rug around her knees, watching the screen.

Suddenly, without moving her eyes from the TV, she said: "I wish I knew why you can't ever look cheerful at home. I'm always hearing people say how cheerful and polite you are. How you're always cracking jokes. But once you come home no one would ever guess."

"Oh, good Lord. I've had a bad day."

She looked at him. "What's the matter, then?"

"You think I can put Frau Wallmann's death behind me just like that? I've known her since she was fifteen, after all. A wonderful woman. You don't meet many like her."

She looked back at the screen. After a while she said, in a thread of a voice: "Sometimes I think you'd rather I'd had an accident and Frau Wallmann was still alive."

He glanced at her. "What do you mean? Don't talk nonsense."

"Oh no, it isn't nonsense. Then you'd still have her to talk to. And you wouldn't have to bother about me any more. And you'd get my fifty thousand marks life insurance too."

Scholten lost his temper. "No, it would be a hundred thousand! You get twice the money when it's accidental death. That's what you'll get yourself if I break my neck."

"Don't say such things, Joseph! What a way to speak to me!"

"What do you mean, what a way to speak to you? You began it."

"I only mentioned poor Frau Wallmann."

"Yes, poor Frau Wallmann! Shall I tell you something? You've been jealous of poor Frau Wallmann from the first, and now she's in her grave you're still jealous of her." To his dismay, Scholten had to suppress a sob. There were tears in his eyes.

"I don't know how you can say a thing like that," said Hilde. "Those are filthy ideas. Why should I have been jealous of poor Frau Wallmann?" She started weeping. "How can you say such things of a dead woman?"

"Oh, bloody hell!" said Scholten in strangulated tones. He got to his feet and went into the kitchen.

"You shouldn't swear!" Hilde called after him. He heard her sobbing.

He went over to the fridge, leaned heavily against it, raised a hand and wiped the tears from his eyes. He shook his head, then opened the fridge and took out a bottle of beer. He raised the bottle to his lips and drank.

Hilde called, "What are you doing out there, Joseph?"

Scholten emptied the bottle before calling back, "I was getting myself a beer." He belched, shook the bottle, held it up close to his eyes.

"What did you say?" she called.

"Nothing."

"Why don't you bring your beer in here and sit down with me?" she called.

He took a second beer from the fridge, went out into the corridor, turned, took a glass out of the kitchen cupboard, went back to the living room. The Bavarian convent was on the TV screen again.

Scholten stared at the television without taking anything in.

If no one had pushed Erika off the steps then they

must have been slippery. Slippery with frost, yes. But Wallmann couldn't have known they would be, not for sure. You don't set up an alibi so carefully for a possibility like that. He had lured her out on the steps, that was obvious, he had made her think she'd be able to catch him down there with his bit of fluff. But the prospect of Erika's falling down the steps just because there was frost on a couple of them was far too unlikely. In fact it was really out of the question. Unless Wallmann had lent a helping hand one way or another.

Scholten gave a start. He sat up very straight, both hands clutching the arms of his chair. Hilde looked at him. He cleared his throat, adjusted the cushion behind his back. Hilde looked back at the screen.

He let himself slowly lean back, suppressing his triumph with difficulty. He'd found the solution, he'd bloody well found the solution! Yes, that's what must have happened: Wallmann had made the steps slippery. He had made them so dangerously slippery that Erika was bound to lose her footing, find nothing to clutch at and fall. And then he'd driven off to set up his alibi.

That was it: that was exactly what he did.

The only question was just how. How do you make wooden steps slippery, very slippery?

With soft soap, like in *It's A Knockout*? No. No, that would have been too dangerous. Wallmann couldn't have taken a risk like that. Soft soap would have stayed on the steps for days, all sticky. Anyone taking a look around up there would have noticed. The police, for instance. The local copper was bound to come up to the house after Wallmann called to say his wife was missing. No, soft soap would have been far too risky for Wallmann.

Unless he had scrubbed the soft soap off again before anyone arrived.

Scholten rubbed his forehead.

It was possible. He'd called the police, reported Erika missing and then gone straight up the steps to scrub the soft soap off. He could easily do it before the local cop arrived. It would probably take the officer a good half hour to get to the house from the village police station.

Scholten put a hand to his ear, rubbed it. All the same, it would still have been quite risky. When had Wallmann returned to the house? Frau Sauerborn had said he left their place at four-thirty exactly. He had driven to the office to fetch his files. He'd have reached the house at around six.

And the steps would have been covered with soft soap from Friday evening until Saturday evening. Anyone could have found it there. Of course, there was a notice in the sandy bay at the bottom of the steps saying *Private Property. Please do not use these steps!* But sometimes people out for a walk did climb them. Scholten himself had once sent two old biddies packing when they suddenly appeared in front of the garage exclaiming: "Oh, isn't it just lovely here!" What a nerve.

The risk would have been damned high.

Scholten poured the rest of the beer into his glass, was about to drink it, then sat there transfixed.

Suddenly he stood up. He went to the living-room cupboard and opened its glass door.

Hilde asked: "What are you looking for?"

He took out a volume of the old encyclopaedia he'd inherited from his Uncle Franz. He said: "There's something I have to look up."

"What do you have to look up?"

He went out of the room. "Back in a moment."

"Why don't you watch the film? It's really good."

He sat down at the kitchen table, opened the volume and leafed hastily through it. Ice, there he was.

Ice, water (q.v.) in its solid aggregate state. The change of water from its liquid to its solid state is described as freezing (q.v.). This occurs as a rule at a temperature of 0 °Celsius (C) or Réamur (R) or +32 °Fahrenheit (F).

"Oh, bloody hell, get to the point," muttered Scholten. He read impatiently on.

He had to read four columns before he found it. *I. is also of great importance in brewing beer (see Ice Cellar).* He looked up "Ice Cellar", but it got him no further. He returned to "Ice", exclaiming "Aha!" when he found the sentence: *Instead of natural ice, however, artificial ice made in ice machines (q.v.) is often used . . .*

He looked up "Ice Machines" and read: *Ice machines, cooling machines, cold machines, machines or devices for producing cold air and cold liquids (for purposes of cooling) and for the artificial manufacturing of ice.*

He sensed that he wasn't going to get anywhere with this either. He made his way through another six columns, glanced at the illustrations, showing an ice machine made in the style of the firm of Vaass & Littmann, Halle. When he came to the section on carbonic acid compressors Hilde said: "What's that you're reading?"

She was standing in the kitchen doorway. He slammed the book shut. "Can't you leave me in peace for five minutes on end?"

"I was leaving you in peace. You've been in here for twenty-five minutes. The film's over. Are you coming to bed?"

Driving home from work on Tuesday, he went to a bookshop. He had been there now and then fetching a book for the project managers, and it was where he had bought Rosie's special anniversary present: *Angélique and the Minister.* He went straight to the technology section and stood around for some time before a longhaired young man approached him.

"Can I help you?"

"I want to buy a book."

"What kind of book?"

"A book about how ice is made."

"Ice?" The young man adjusted his glasses.

"Yes, ice. Don't you understand that? A book about how to make ice, it's perfectly simple."

"You mean ice cream?"

"No, no, not ice cream. I mean how do you make real ice?"

"Well, in the fridge, I should think. Or the freezer."

"I know. Are you trying to be funny?"

"No, certainly not. I'll try to find out for you."

"My God, you're slow on the uptake. I am looking for a book describing the way ice is made."

The young man adjusted his glasses again. "Excuse me, I am not slow on the uptake, but you don't express yourself very clearly. Do you mean a description of an ice machine?"

"No, I don't. I can find all that in the encyclopaedia."

"Then I really don't know what you're after."

Scholten struggled for words for a moment. Then he said, "Kiss my arse" and walked out of the shop.

He tried again. On Wednesday evening he stopped by a phone box on the way home and called Frings the journalist. He asked if the Met Office could tell you how to make ice. Frings asked questions until it was clear what Scholten wanted to know: whether ice could be made in the open air. An artificial layer of ice on a road, for instance? Yes, that was right, on a road. Or on steps. Say on the steps up to the cathedral.

Frings said he couldn't imagine it. It would be impossible. Of course you could pour water over the road or down the cathedral steps, but it wouldn't freeze unless everywhere else around had a temperature at freezing point. You'd need, as it were, to build a huge fridge over the road or round the cathedral steps. "But that would surely be rather expensive, don't you think, Herr Höffner?"

Scholten really wanted to ask Frings how he could be so certain, and wouldn't it be better to call the Met Office before handing out information? But he gave up. He said, "Well, thanks very much, then," hung up the receiver, said "Bastard," and drove home.

Two days later, on Good Friday afternoon when Scholten was sitting watching television with Hilde, a performance of the *St Matthew Passion*, he gave up the ice idea. Another and much better solution had suddenly occurred to him in a flash of inspiration: Wallmann had stretched threads across the steps!

Scholten almost jumped up to fetch his drawing from the desk. But he controlled himself. Hilde would have been upset, and the music really was beautiful. He didn't need the drawing either. He could see the wooden steps quite clearly in his mind's eye: the stringboards of the flight of steps sloping vertically down, framing and supporting the planks that acted as the steps themselves. Every plank rested on two strong, long angle-irons screwed to the right and left of the inside of the wooden stringboards. And each plank was fixed to its angle-irons by bolts, one on the right and one on the left.

The stringboards of the steps rose a few inches above

the planks on both sides. Wallmann had only to knock a nail into the top of the stringboards to right and left, three or four inches above the plank, and tie cords between them.

Erika came down the steps, stumbled over one of the cords and fell. Perhaps there was a little frost on the wood too, and she couldn't catch hold of anything to break her fall.

That's how it must have been.

Scholten rubbed his forehead. There was a certain amount of risk still involved, of course. Yes, it had definitely been risky; Wallmann couldn't remove the cords until Saturday evening. And someone might have seen them before then.

But who'd go up there, at this time of the year too?

Anyway, cords would have been much less conspicuous than soft soap. And there'd be nothing to scrub off. He could have torn the cords away in a few seconds.

That was just how it had been. It must be. And now, at last, everything fitted together. The christening, Wallmann's alibi. The files. It all made sense.

Scholten gradually relaxed. He let himself sit back in his armchair. After a while he began humming along with the music: *O Mensch, bewein dein Sünde gross* . . . His eyes filled with tears. The goddamned bastard.

Scholten gritted his teeth.

On Easter Saturday he went to confession with Hilde. She took his arm as they walked to church and said she could feel a change in the weather. Dark ragged clouds were racing over the bright sky. Gusts of warm wind blew. She said she'd felt it last night too. The bare branches of the trees bent in the wind.

After a while she said: "Why don't you say anything?"

"Me?"

"Yes, who else?"

"I was thinking."

"What about?"

"What about!" He pushed his hat more firmly down on his forehead. "Don't you ever think before going to confession?"

"Oh, well, I didn't know you were doing that. If it's your confession you're thinking about, then I'll say no more. You don't need to say anything either."

"No, I don't."

After a while she added: "You do know you don't just have to confess the things you've actually done, don't you?"

"What's that supposed to mean?"

"You have to confess the bad thoughts you've had too."

"Yes, right."

As they climbed the steps to the church door she said: "If you've suspected anyone unjustly, then you have to confess that as well."

He held the church door open for her and said: "Oh, do drop the subject. Do you think I don't know how to confess?"

She whispered sharply: "Keep your voice down."

Scholten helped her as she kneeled down in the pew. She buried her face in both hands.

The twilit silence of the church affected him. He moved his lips and turned his eyes to the dark red of the Eternal Light.

Suddenly there was a loud crash. Someone had stumbled over a pew or dropped a prayer book. Scholten looked round and shook his head disapprovingly.

He went into the confessional after Hilde. She had passed him with eyes lowered and hands clasped over her breast. In the dim light behind the curtain,

Scholten dropped to his knees. After the opening formula he said: "I have committed the sin of unchastity." He hesitated for a moment and then said: "Alone and with others."

The priest behind the thin wooden screen sighed. He asked how old Scholten was, whether he was married, and how often it had happened. Scholten gave a rough estimate, saying it had been with various women, at intervals, in a brothel.

The priest said that at his age Scholten really should be learning to deal with temptation. He asked if he had anything else to confess.

Scholten thought of Wallmann's cigars, but that was only petty theft of consumables. He said: "No, that's all."

The priest said it was quite enough and urged him to mend his ways. He might think, added the priest, of the pain his wife would feel if she knew what he got up to.

As penance he gave him five Our Fathers and five Hail Marys to say.

Scholten duly said them, and after a while, when his thoughts had wandered off again, he added an extra Our Father. He asked the Lord to help him bring that bastard Wallmann to justice. He concluded with another Hail Mary too.

The steps. He must go and look at those steps as soon as possible. For heaven's sake, there must be some kind of evidence he could find there! That goddamned bastard couldn't get away with it.

10

The week after Easter passed, and Scholten was getting very restless. He had hoped Wallmann would send him up to the weekend house again soon. In autumn Wallmann had said the deck of the boat would have to be painted in spring, and Scholten had mentioned that the shutters would want some attention by then too. And by this time there'd be a fine crop of weeds round the house; they grew like mad up there in the middle of the woods.

But Wallmann did not suggest sending him over.

Scholten wondered whether to ask if he should go. But that was too risky. Wallmann might get suspicious. Or he might say no just to spite him.

When yet another week had passed, Scholten came to a decision. On Wednesday afternoon he suddenly stood up, clutched his stomach and ran to the lavatory. When he came back Rosa Thelen said: "Anything wrong with you?"

"I don't know. I suddenly got such cramps in my stomach. Diarrhoea too."

"What have you eaten?"

"Only my sandwich at lunch. But perhaps there was something the matter with the beer. It did taste rather odd." He put his hands to his belly.

Five minutes later he went to the lavatory again. When he came back Rosa had been into the project managers' office to ask if anyone else was feeling unwell.

Rothgerber came into the filing room, looked at Scholten and said: "What is it, then? Got the trots? Have some of my schnapps."

"Schnapps is pure poison for that kind of thing!" said Rosa indignantly. "I'll make him some tea."

Rothgerber said: "That'll just make him feel even worse. What kind of tea?"

"Camomile."

Scholten uttered a suppressed groan, clutched his stomach and went off to the lavatory again. Meanwhile Kurowski was already inspecting all the beer bottles from the crate in the storeroom. As Scholten left the lavatory, he was standing in the doorway of the office building, holding a bottle up to the light. He said: "Scholten's right. This one's cloudy. I don't think I'm feeling too good either."

Inge Faust was standing in the filing room, watching Rosa Thelen make tea. When Scholten came in she said: "Herr Scholten, you'd better go home. There's no point staying at work if you have to keep running to the toilet."

Scholten sat down at his desk. "No, that's all right, it'll pass off. It wasn't quite as bad just now." He busied himself with his papers.

Inge Faust marched over to Wallmann's office. Two minutes later Wallmann left the building. Out in the corridor he said, raising his voice: "So where would we be if everyone went off sick just because he was shitting himself?" He got into his car and drove off.

Kurowski, on his way to the door with another couple of bottles, came into the filing room and said: "I tell you what, if I was you I'd shit right here in the middle of the corridor. That man's crazy. You go home. He can't do anything to you."

Scholten dismissed the idea. "No, no, he's right. I've never gone off work for something like that."

He stayed until the office closed. He drank three cups of camomile tea and went to the lavatory another six times. As he took his coat from his locker Wallmann came out into the corridor and said: "Are you ill?"

"Oh, it's not too bad. Stomach cramps. And I feel a bit weak now, but that's not surprising."

"You'd better stay at home tomorrow, then."

"Oh, well – it must have been the beer. The bottle I drank had probably gone off."

"Could be. Or then again you might have something infectious. Stay at home tomorrow, and if you're still unwell on Friday call and say so."

"Well, maybe that's a good idea. Before I pass any bugs on to everyone else. But I'll definitely be back on Friday, or I'll have too much to catch up with."

He began worrying on his way home. What would he do if Inge Faust or Rosa called him at home tomorrow to ask how he was? Either of them easily might.

Next morning he left home at his usual time, five to six. Hilde, in her dressing gown, held the door slightly ajar and watched him go. He waved to her as he reached the landing of the stairs and went on down and immediately realized that it was a mistake. She would notice. She'd wonder why he waved.

As he joined the motorway he felt fear like a lump in his belly. There was a good deal of traffic on the motorway at this time of day. And some idiots drove like scalded pigs. If he had an accident here there really would be hell to pay. He clutched the steering wheel. Then he tried to adopt a relaxed position. Take it slowly, Jupp Scholten. We have plenty of time.

He felt relieved when he could turn off the motor-way and join the ordinary road. There was hardly anyone driving in the same direction, and traffic coming the other way was light. Once he had passed the small town, and the road began winding its way up into the hills, no other vehicles at all met him. The sun had risen above the woods, the meadows sparkled with dew. Scholten wound down the window and let in the fresh morning air.

But the hardest part still lay ahead. He turned off the main road sooner than usual, took a circuitous route along minor roads, through spruce woods where the light was still dim, and did not approach Wallmann's weekend retreat from the usual direction. If he had driven through the village, Grandmontagne might have seen him, or Grandmontagne's wife, or Hückelhoven the baker, or the Widow Abels. The whole village knew him, and his car too.

One or two miles before reaching the track that led to the path along the banks of the lake, he turned into a clearing. Take it easy, Jupp Scholten, take it very easy. We have plenty of time. It was a quarter to eight. He drove the car to one side so that it couldn't be seen from the road. He got out and looked around him. No one in sight, no sound but the twittering of the birds.

He went to the road and looked right and left. Then he crossed it, searched around for a dry place, jumped the ditch and slipped, saved himself from falling with both hands. His right hand met mud. He wiped it off on the grass. Take it easy, Jupp Scholten.

He crossed the wood at an angle. Dead twigs broke under his shoes. Twice he didn't bend down far enough, and his hat was almost swept off his head; he straightened it again. He was feeling warm in his coat. As he reached the path along the banks he felt sweat break out between his shoulder blades.

He unbuttoned the coat, took a deep breath. Ducks

were quacking among the reeds by the bank. The lake lay broad and calm. Only occasionally did a little wave run towards the bank, break and flow back. The blue western sky stood above the tall trees on the little promontory to his left. A faint mist enveloped the black humpbacked wooded land on the far side of the lake.

Scholten turned right. He followed the winding path along the bank. He took his hat off, wiped his forehead and neck with his handkerchief. A light wind blew over the reeds. When Scholten reached the end of the path he stopped, got behind a tree and looked out over the little sandy bay. No one in sight. The concert of birdsong continued, interrupted only by tiny pauses at irregular intervals.

The boat was rocking on the water by the landing stage. Scholten saw the bottom of the steps on the opposite side of the sandy bay. The morning sun shone down on their grey planks. His lips moving silently, he counted the bottom steps up to the landing, where the flight disappeared from view behind the steep bank. Fourteen planks.

Scholten breathed in deeply. Right, here we go. He walked down to the sandy bay, looked around him once more then took his coat off as he walked on. He hung it over a projecting rock on the bank, with his jacket over it and his hat on top of them. He wondered whether to take his pullover off too. No, the wind was freshening, as it always did at this time of day.

Scholten went up the steps, one hand on the birch tree trunk that did duty as a handrail. On the landing he was about to kneel down but then shook his head. "Come on, take it easy, Jupp Scholten. Take a look at the house first." He went up the last five steps and, looking all round him, went to the space behind the garage. "Some bloody fool with no business here could be poking around. Or some nosy old woman. Go carefully, Jupp Scholten. You have to be a hundred per cent sure with this kind of thing."

The gravel crunched underfoot. Scholten bent down and pulled out a few of the green shoots coming up between the little stones. "He should have sent me up here last week. But it's all the same to him. He has more important things to do."

He looked round the corner of the garage at the forecourt in front of it. He walked once round the house, shaking a shutter here and there, pulling out a weed now and then. He stopped in front of one of the shutters, scratched the paint with a fingernail. "About time too." He put both hands on his hips and looked at the thin flakes of colour coming away.

A jay screeched, very close. Scholten jumped. "Stupid bird."

Slowly he went down the five steps to the landing, took a deep breath. "Here we go, then. And you watch out, Wallmann." He kneeled down, passed his hand over the stringboards of the steps. He thrust his head forward, narrowed his eyes.

Nothing to be seen.

He straightened up, thought. Of course, Wallmann would have been crazy just to take the cords away and leave the nails in the wood. Naturally he took the nails out too. It wouldn't have taken him long.

Scholten peered closely at the left-hand stringboard of the steps, inspecting it bit by bit. He couldn't find any nail-marks level with the last step before the landing, or above the next plank either. He felt sweat gathering above his eyebrows.

Straightening up again, he groaned and passed the back of his hand over his brow. He ought to have brought a magnifying glass. No, that was nonsense. Wallmann couldn't have tied the cords to drawing pins; Erika would simply have pulled those out. They must have been good strong nails.

Scholten bent down again. He found a nail-mark in the stringboard above the second plank from the top. He immediately looked at the stringboard on the opposite side, but he found nothing there. He took a deep breath.

The nail didn't have to have been exactly level with the one opposite. He searched the cracked wood of the stringboard from top to bottom, bit by bit. But he found nothing.

Half-lying, he propped himself on the steps, looking straight ahead. As he searched for his handkerchief he heard a distant cry. He jumped in alarm, looked around. A yacht came sailing along the lake, tacking in the wind. The mainsail hid the crew.

Panic-stricken, Scholten thought of going up to the house, but then he remembered his coat. He hurried down the steps, looking over his shoulder, snatched up his hat, coat and jacket and ran over the sand of the bay, bending low.

When he was behind the trees the yacht turned and began running before the wind. A woman in a yellow jacket was sitting at the tiller; a man was crouching in the boat. They were both looking straight ahead.

Scholten mopped the sweat from his brow. He stood there for a good ten minutes until the yacht, now very far away, had disappeared around the next promontory. Slowly he went back.

There was no real point in it any more. The idea of the cords couldn't be right. The nails would have left marks in the stringboards of the steps.

He stood there in the bay, his hat on his head, his

coat and jacket over his arm. He gritted his teeth. Bastard. Oh, you bloody bastard.

After a while he moved towards the steps. He turned, put his coat and jacket down behind a tree. Then he climbed the steps one by one, very slowly. He stopped on the landing. He stared at the steps above it. He rubbed his brow and shook his head.

Suddenly he bent down. He ran his thumb over the front edge of the first plank above the landing. Then he kneeled down, but finding that he couldn't get his eyes close enough to the plank in that position he lay flat on the landing of the flight of steps. He put his eyes very close to the front edge of the plank, rubbed his thumb over the wood again.

Hope stirred in him.

11

There was no doubt about it. Those were fresh nail-marks. The nails had been knocked into the front of the plank forming the tread of the step, four of them side by side at intervals of about six inches, almost exactly in the middle of the wood. They had been good strong nails.

Scholten sat down on the landing, rubbed both hands over his face. He looked at the steps to his left. Then he found the same marks in the second plank above the landing. Four fresh nail-holes at roughly the same distance from each other.

He became extremely excited, moving so impulsively that he caught his trousers on a splinter on the landing and pulled a thread out. He took no notice, got down on all fours and crawled up the steps, plank by plank.

Nothing else came to light. There were no marks on the top three planks. The nails had been only in the two directly above the landing, four nails in each of them.

Scholten sat on the top step. He looked out at the lake, but he did not see the blue water, the calm and shallow waves that the wind blew before it, he did not see the glittering reflections of the sun or the mist blurring the outline of the opposite bank.

He was certain that he was on Wallmann's trail now. But he still couldn't make sense of his discovery.

Nails in the fronts of the steps; you couldn't fix

anything in those to make a really effective mantrap. You could, of course, stretch cords up and down, from plank to plank. And perhaps someone might catch a foot in them. But if the death-trap was to function at all reliably, if someone was to stumble over them and fall, then the cords would have to be stretched lengthways. And above the planks, not along their front edges.

Scholten struck the palm of his left hand with his clenched right fist again and again. The bastard, the goddamned bloody bastard! It must be possible to find out what he'd been up to somehow!

He rose ponderously, stood there for a moment and then went slowly down the steps. He turned on the second step and climbed down backwards, very slowly, running his eyes over the planks one by one. He counted the eight nail-holes, but he found nothing else.

He did not stay on the landing but went on climbing backwards down the steps. His eyes were already inspecting the next step when he froze. He leaned well forward.

Yes. The outside plank of the landing had nail-holes in it too. Four of them again, below the edge of the plank at intervals of about six inches from each other.

He straightened up and examined the landing. It consisted of three planks fitted side by side. They were set at an angle to the five upper planks, the steps leading up to the space behind the garage. The planks of the landing were fitted in the same direction as the fourteen steps below it that went down to the sandy bay.

Scholten ran his hand under the outside plank. He could feel the nut of the bolt fixing the plank to the angle-iron. The nut was very smooth. He withdrew his hand and looked at it. There were traces of grease on his fingertips.

He felt for the bolt on the opposite side. Its shank and the nut were smooth too.

Scholten inspected his fingertips. Suddenly he lay flat on the landing again. His hat fell off; he caught it and put it down on a step. He felt for the bolts under the two planks above the landing, putting his head as close as possible to get a clearer view of the nuts and the shanks of the bolts.

There was no doubt about it: those bolts had been greased not long ago too.

Scholten propped one arm on the landing. He was breathing heavily. He looked over his shoulder at the lake. The triangular sails of two yachts were moving past the opposite bank. A few white clouds stood above the hilly outline of the woods, very far away.

He took a couple of deep breaths and then lowered himself again. He tried undoing the nuts with his fingers. It was difficult; they were quite tightly screwed on. He thought of going back to the car for his monkey wrench, but he was too impatient.

He managed without a tool. His thumb and forefinger were left sore and bleeding, but after a good half hour he had taken out the two planks above the landing and the three planks of the landing itself. There was now a large hole yawning in the flight of steps. He had carried the planks down the steps one by one and put them on the landing stage.

After carrying the last plank down he sat on the landing stage and dangled his legs. He wiped his thumb and forefinger with his handkerchief, licked the wounds. He rubbed his forehead and neck dry. Then he stood up and examined the planks again, one by one.

When he took the planks out he had discovered something that couldn't be coincidence, couldn't be mere chance: each of the five had nail-marks not just in front but all the way round the edges. There had been four nails on each of the long sides and two on each of the narrow sides. And all the marks were still fresh.

And the bolts holding those planks to the angle-irons on the left and the right of the stringboards had all recently been greased. The grease was still pale and soft.

There was only one explanation: Wallmann had done it. He had taken the five planks out, knocked the nails into their sides and greased the nuts and bolts.

But why? Scholten looked up at the hole in the steps. Yes, if Erika had gone down to it she'd have lost her footing. That had been his first idea: Wallmann had simply removed the five planks and Erika fell through the hole.

But he immediately had reservations about that explanation.

The risk to Wallmann would have been too great. Such a huge hole in the steps was too conspicuous. Anyway, the nails didn't fit a plan like that. Why would Wallmann have knocked the nails in if he were only going to remove the planks? It made no sense.

Yes. Why had he knocked those nails in? In all, twelve of them around each plank.

Scholten stared up at the hole in the flight of steps. Suddenly he felt hot. For God's sake, if someone came along now hiding would be no use at all. That hole could be seen even from the water.

He glanced quickly at the lake. A yacht was tacking against the wind not very far away. He took the first plank and ran up the steps.

Twenty minutes later he had reassembled the five planks. He had tightened the nuts as well as he could with his sore fingers, swearing out loud now and then.

He sat on the landing of the steps and stretched his legs. The yacht had turned away. He dabbed at his injuries and licked them. They hurt like hell. He looked at his watch. Oh, Christ, past twelve already.

Just before one, Scholten stopped at a village pub. A very fat young woman came out of the kitchen. He asked if he could have lunch there. The fat woman said she could do him a schnitzel and fried potatoes. He ordered a side salad too, drank three beers and a cup of coffee. He selected a black cigar.

Around three-thirty Scholten reached the motorway ring road round the city. He threw the stub of the cigar that he had been chewing out of the window and started to sing. A snatch from the *St Matthew Passion*, but he didn't know how it went on. He changed to a cheerful dialect song, and then he chanted: "Wallmann, Wallmann, just you wait . . ."

He drove to the brothel. The woman he chose after a short inspection did her job very well. She was friendly too. When he was lying on top of her she even smiled at him.

Soon after four-thirty Scholten parked outside the front door of his building. As he got out of the car a heavy weight seemed to descend on him; what was he going to say if Rosa Thelen or Inge Faust had called to ask how he was?

He'd meant to think something up, but he had entirely forgotten.

He wondered whether to walk round the block thinking up a story and then tell Hilde he'd been kept late at work. No, that wouldn't do. She was probably standing at the window; she'd have seen him already.

Suddenly fury overcame him. He opened the front door and climbed the stairs. As he reached the first floor he said out loud: "Does this place always have to stink so bad?"

Hilde was already in the doorway of the apartment. She said: "Who was that you were talking to?"

"No one."

"No one? You were talking so loud to no one?"

"That's right."

She closed the door. "What's the matter with you?"

"Me? Why would anything be the matter with me? Maybe something's the matter with you."

"Me? Well, there isn't." Her voice was very thin.

He felt calmer. Obviously no one had called. He said: "Yes, well, never mind. I've had a busy day, I'm feeling a bit edgy."

"Just edgy? Or aren't you feeling well?"

"No, no, I'm fine."

"Then you go and sit down." She hesitated and then said: "Maybe you'd like a beer?"

"Yes, indeed, a beer might do me good." He went into the kitchen, sniffed. "What's for supper, then?"

"Curly kale and smoked sausage."

"Delicious."

The cat came and rubbed around his legs. He bent down and stroked the animal. "There now, good little Manny. So what have you been doing today? Come along and tell me."

12

He did not manage to solve his problem over the weekend, although he thought about it in every free minute Hilde allowed him. It simply made no sense to take those five planks out, hammer nails in all round them and then remove the nails again and fit the planks back into the steps. Something was missing from the chain of events. But what? Perhaps he had missed seeing something. Or perhaps it was hidden in the house: a clue, the missing link that would fit everything together and make sense of it.

He had to get into the house as soon as possible and look around. But suppose the bastard didn't send him over there at all? Perhaps he'd found someone else for the odd jobs?

At midday on Monday Wallmann looked in at the filing room when he came back from the building sites. Rosa had gone out. Scholten was just in time to hide the copy of *Der Spiegel* that Rothgerber had lent him.

Wallmann said: "Herr Scholten, if this weather holds, maybe you could drive up to the house by the lake this week and paint the shutters."

It was with difficulty that Scholten hid his glee. He looked out of the window, said, "Yes, fine," and nodded.

"Or would you rather not?"

"What's that got to do with it? It's high time those shutters were painted. Didn't you want the deck of the boat done too?"

"I'll have to supervise the deck myself. But the mainsail will need cleaning. You could do that."

"And something should be done about the weeds," said Scholten. "But I can't do it all in a day."

"I'm not asking you to. Why not drive up there on Thursday and stay overnight? And if you're not through with it by Friday evening you can finish the job on Saturday morning. I'll pay."

"Well, yes, but that's difficult because of my wife. I mean, I can't leave her alone that long. And then I have to go shopping on Saturday."

Wallmann hesitated briefly. Then he said: "Why not take your wife with you?"

Scholten shifted in his chair. "No, I couldn't do that," he said. "It would get her too agitated. She can't take that kind of thing."

"Well, I expect you know best."

Scholten said: "But maybe I could drive up on Wednesday. Then I'd have until Friday evening to do the job. That's still two nights, of course . . ."

Wallmann said: "I'll pay." He took out his wallet, removed two hundred-mark notes from it, added a fifty and put the money down on Scholten's desk.

"Yes, fine," said Scholten. "Thanks very much."

Wallmann said: "You can go and buy the paint and stuff this afternoon if you like. Or tomorrow morning. Come into my office afterwards, and we'll think what else you need."

Scholten left the office at three and drove to the DIY store. He bought paint and turpentine substitute, a couple of paintbrushes and a scrubbing brush. He wheeled his laden trolley into the car park and stowed everything into the boot of his car. Then he looked around. He hid one of the two hundred-mark notes that he had already put in his coat pocket under the mat inside the boot.

He said nothing about it to Hilde that evening. When he came home on Tuesday evening he was already muttering to himself on the stairs. As he hung his coat and jacket on the coat-rack he cleared his throat loudly several times.

Hilde asked: "Is anything wrong?"

He grunted, went into the bedroom and put his slippers on. She followed him. "What's the matter?"

He shook his head. "Oh, just feeling annoyed. I don't want to do it, but I have to go up to the house by the lake again this week."

"Herr Wallmann's weekend house?"

"Yes, where else? The shutters need painting."

"And you have to go up just for that? You're not a painter at Herr Wallmann's beck and call! Why don't you tell him no?"

"Tell him no? Just like that? And how about the money? We just say no to the money, do we?"

"Why are you always going on about money? We can manage. There's no need to have everything." Her voice turned not thin but sharp. "How much is he paying you?"

"A hundred and fifty marks. He's given it to me in advance."

"That's ridiculous. He'd have to pay twice or three times that for a painter."

"Go on, you don't believe that yourself. It's just for two days. And I'm getting my salary at the same time."

"What did you say? Two days? You mean you're going to stay overnight?"

He went into the kitchen, with Hilde on his heels. He took a bottle of beer out of the fridge. "I'm driving over tomorrow evening straight from the office. So that I can get things ready and make an early start on Thursday. I won't get it done in the time otherwise. I'll be back on Friday."

"You're going away tomorrow evening? That's two nights!"

"Yes, I said so. I tell you, I won't get it done in the time otherwise."

"This is unbelievable! You're doing it just so you can go to Grandmontagne's bar tomorrow evening. And on Thursday too."

"Oh, rubbish. Anyway, Granmontansch's is closed on Thursdays."

"Don't say Granmontansch. Why don't you ever listen to what I tell you? It's pronounced Graamontanya."

"Yes, yes, I know you passed your school-leaving exams. But everyone in the village says Granmontansch, and they should know. I mean, he's not a Belgian."

She said: "That's got nothing to do with it."

He drank his beer while she cast about for a new approach. He asked: "What's for supper?"

"Smoked pork loin and sauerkraut."

"Delicious." But he knew they hadn't exhausted the subject yet. He sat down at the kitchen table in front of the plate she had already put out for him. Sitting opposite, cutting her pork into small pieces, she said: "I know you like going up there."

"Are you starting on about that again?"

"Who knows what you do there?"

"Oh, sure, I have all the village women come up to the house."

"Don't be so crude."

"Me? It was you thinking something crude, that's what."

"No, I was not. That's a dreadful thing to say."

94

"What were you thinking, then?"

She toyed with her sauerkraut. Then she said: "You want to go up there because then you can be away from me for two days and two nights." Her face twisted. "I'd be better off dead."

"Oh, for God's sake!"

"Don't swear!"

He flung his fork down on the plate. "Shall I tell you something? I have to take what I can get, understand? Frau Wallmann isn't there now. And that fellow is unpredictable, see? Last week I had diarrhoea, and Fräulein Faust told him I ought to go home. You should have heard how he carried on."

"When did you have diarrhoea?"

He went on eating. "Oh, never mind. I'm just telling you, that man's unpredictable. He could easily sack me. And then what? At fifty-eight I'll be on the dole. I won't find another job, not like the one I've got now."

She was still toying with her sauerkraut. She said: "I've told you often enough, you ought to have looked around for a good profession. And a good training."

He waved his fork in the air. "So how? Just how?"

"I told you so in 1947 when you were back from POW camp. I even said so in 1943 when we met. But I expect you've forgotten."

"Yes, I know, everything was different in Breslau and much better. People in Breslau took their school-leaving exams."

"You could have taken them too."

He waved his fork again. "Didn't I tell you, my father took me out of secondary school because he couldn't pay the fees? He was just a postal worker, it was hard for him to find twenty marks a month." Scholten felt his eyes watering. "He didn't want to take me out of school, believe me. He wanted me to do well in life. But he had no alternative."

She looked at her plate. She said: "No, because you had to stay down a year."

He looked at her, eyes still watering. Then he abruptly put a forkful of sauerkraut in his mouth and chewed it in silence.

She took a piece of pork and masticated, keeping her eyes fixed on her plate. She said: "That was it, wasn't it? If you'd worked harder you could have got a scholarship. I got a scholarship. So did my brother. But you had no ambition." He looked at her. She chewed and said nothing. Two tears welled out of his eyes. He wiped them away.

She didn't look at him. She took another piece of pork and said: "You've never in your life had any ambition. That's why you have to let Herr Wallmann order you about at the age of fifty-eight."

He scraped his plate clean, put the fork in his mouth, replaced it on the plate. He rose and went out. He went to the bathroom, where he bolted the door, took out his handkerchief and blew his nose. He looked in the mirror and wiped his eyes, but more tears kept coming.

He sat down on the lavatory and wept. He pressed his handkerchief to his mouth to muffle the sound of his sobs. After a while, amidst tears, he said into his handkerchief: "One of these days I'll murder you yet."

13

The weather was still warm and sunny. When Scholten got out of his car outside Wallmann's weekend house on Wednesday evening he stretched, reached his arms out, took a deep breath. The first hint of twilight was descending over the trees, but the birds were still awake. Scholten drank in the smell of the conifers, bushes and grasses. He imitated a bird's voice and then called into the woods, "Go on, you can sing a little more! I like to hear you, birds!"

He cleared the boot of the car, took the cans of paint into the garage. After making up the guestroom bed with clean sheets he stood in the hall for a moment, undecided. He would have liked to begin his investigations straight away. He looked in at the living room, opened a drawer.

"Nonsense. We have two whole days, Jupp Scholten."

He got into his car and drove down to the village.

Grandmontagne was sitting at the regulars' table with the corner seat, in the company of the Widow Abels, Palm the grocer and his son Karl-Heinz who worked on the railway, the farmers Quademichels and Laudenberg, and Käthchen Hückelhoven, the baker's wife. Grandmontagne's wife was behind the bar.

When Scholten came in Grandmontagne cried: "Hey, look at this, then. Old Jupp's back!" Scholten shook hands, sat down between Palm and the Widow Abels, and ordered a plate of sliced cold meat and sauerkraut from Frau Grandmontagne. "With plenty of onion!"

"It's all right for him, he sleeps alone!" Käthchen Hückelhoven commented.

Grandmontagne said: "That's what you think. Well, we don't none of us know what goes on in that house. Old Jupp knows his way around."

Scholten bought a round to celebrate being back in the village. They wanted to know what Herr Wallmann was doing these days and how the business was going without Frau Wallmann and what the funeral had been like. Karl-Heinz Palm and Laudenberg, who were both in the volunteer fire brigade, told him about the search for the body and how they found it.

Grandmontagne examined the stem of his beer glass, smiled, moved the glass back and forth. "You got no idea what really happened."

Laudenberg became heated. "What d'you mean? You wasn't there. You was watching Alemannia play that Sunday. We was freezing our arses off down by the lake while you was sitting in the stands with your hip-flask."

Grandmontagne leaned over the table. "So who did the cops come to see? The CID? You or me?" He leaned back again. "There you are."

Scholten put a piece of sausage in his mouth and said: "You don't say. You mean the CID came to see you?"

"On the Tuesday, that was. But it really began Saturday, with Kreutzer."

Scholten masticated. "Kreutzer, that's the village copper?"

Hückelhoven the baker, who had come in and sat down in the meantime, said: "Call Kreutzer a copper, and he'll smash your face in. Officer Kreutzer, that's him."

Quademichels puffed his pipe. "Officer Kreutzer? He's too dopey for a cop."

Grandmontagne said: "Look, do you want to hear how it was or don't you?"

"Ssh," said the Widow Abels. "Let's hear it. How about another little round, Marlene?"

Grandmontagne lowered his voice. "Well, Wallmann must have been real pissed off with Kreutzer."

"Why?"

"Because Kreutzer didn't raise the alarm at once. Didn't fancy looking for the body."

Karl-Heinz Palm reached over the table and clapped Laudenberg on the shoulder. "See? I told you it were Kreutzer's fault, I did. Seeing as the woman was drunk Friday, they could have gone looking for her Saturday."

Laudenberg rubbed his shoulder in annoyance. "Rubbish! He never noticed his wife was missing till Saturday evening. We wouldn't never have found her in the night."

"Oh no? So how about that bloke we fished out two years back? That were two in the morning, that were."

"He were pissed as a newt, that bloke. You didn't have to do nowt but take a look from the fisherman's hut by the moorings, you could bring him in straight off."

Grandmontagne raised his voice. "That's not the point!"

"How come?"

"That bloke near the fisherman's hut was paralytic, there had to be a search right away. Seeing as anyone could guess he wouldn't've made it round the curve when he come up to the moorings."

"So how about the woman, then?"

"Well, she weren't drunk, let's get that clear. I seen

her here half an hour before she died, sitting at this very table she was, right where Quademichels is sitting this very minute."

Quademichels felt uncomfortable. All eyes were turned to him. He didn't know where to look.

Karl-Heinz Palm said: "Look, I done that meself, getting tight in half an hour ain't no problem."

His father dug him in the ribs. "You shut your gob. Stop talking so daft."

Grandmontagne raised his forefinger. "If a kid goes missing then the cops got to be told at once. Or a nutcase, or a drunk. They got to look for that sort straight away. But with a woman like her, well, that's different, innit?"

"Why's it different?"

"The police don't have no clear guidelines. It's called 'missing adults'. And if a missing adult disappears there ain't no call to go looking for them straight off."

Frau Grandmontagne came in with the tray and handed round the glasses. She took one herself and said "Thanks," raising her glass to the Widow Abels. Then Hückelhoven wiped the froth from his moustache and said to Grandmontagne: "I don't believe that. How come you know all this?"

"Got it from Kreutzer."

Quademichels saw a chance to make his point again. He said: "He's too dopey for a cop."

Grandmontagne raised his voice a little. "That ain't got nothing to do with it! Do *you* know all the laws? And the decrees and all that stuff?"

Quademichels blinked uncertainly and puffed at his pipe.

Grandmontagne said: "Right, so Kreutzer come up here yesterday. He told me all about it. In this here

100

country adults can go where they like, see? The law says so. Even a married woman can. She don't even need to tell her husband."

The Widow Abels laughed, leaned forward and said: "Hear that, Käthchen?"

Hückelhoven said: "That's what the SPD does for you. Didn't never used to be like that."

Scholten moved slightly away from the warm thigh of the Widow Abels and looked at Grandmontagne. "What do you mean, Sheng?"

"Clear as day, innit? Could be Frau Wallmann was planning to run off. Could be she had a boyfriend somewhere, she was going to see him. And there ain't a thing the police can do about that. The law says so."

"Don't talk such nonsense! That's insulting the memory of the dead!" Scholten pointed his forefinger at Grandmontagne. "I'll tell you something: I've known that woman since she was fifteen. She was quality. No question. She wouldn't run off, not her!"

Käthchen Hückelhoven said: "What do you mean, quality? That don't mean she had to put up with everything. Her old man gets around, right? Anyone can see that. And if he do what he likes, why shouldn't she have a bit on the side too?"

Scholten slammed his hand down on the table. "Because she didn't! I know that for certain! And I won't have you call her names!"

Grandmontagne said: "Hey, don't get so worked up, Jupp. I never said Frau Wallmann had any boyfriend."

"Well, she didn't."

"I only said Kreutzer didn't *have* to go looking straight off. On account of it says not in the guidelines. He didn't know nothing about the lady, he didn't know her from Eve. And he says so to Wallmann when

101

Wallmann calls on Saturday evening, and that's when Wallmann gets so worked up."

"I'd've felt the same," said Palm.

"Me too," said Quademichels. "If my wife was to run off . . ." He nodded, sought for words. He drew on his pipe. Then he said: "Well, there'd be trouble."

Karl-Heinz Palm nudged him in the ribs. "You wasn't listening proper again."

Quademichels blinked. "What?"

Grandmontagne said: "Another round here, Marlene."

Käthchen Hückelhoven was not at all happy. She said: "That man's a real goer, he is. Him and his yacht."

"What's that s'posed to mean?" Hückelhoven leaned forward and looked sharply at his wife. "Why's he a goer just because he got a yacht?"

"Go on with you, Fritz," said Laudenberg and laughed. "He knows his way around, he do. I seen that boat of 'is by the fisherman's hut that Thursday evening. Probably taking summat aboard for the night. Must be good on a boat, I bet. You don't need to do nothing, it go up and down by itself."

The widow said: "Ooh, you're so crude, Hubert."

"Which Thursday?" asked Scholten.

"Day before his wife breaks her neck, that were."

"He was at the fisherman's hut then?"

"Yeah, his boat were tied up near the bridge. I didn't see him, though. I didn't go in."

"You don't half surprise me," said Käthchen Hückelhoven.

Scholten, who had been staring at the table, looked at Grandmontagne and said: "So how about the CID? The cops?"

"Oh, yeah, I can tell you all about that."

"And we all heard it already too," said Hückelhoven. "You told it at least three times."

"But Jupp here ain't heard it."

The Widow Abels said: "Let Sheng tell it again, then. You don't get summat like this happen every day." She settled herself comfortably on the corner seat, and Scholten felt the warm pressure of her thigh again. He hesitated for a moment and then returned it. The widow smiled and stayed put.

Grandmontagne said: "Well, so the cops was here the Tuesday after the accident. Two of 'em. And I gets the impression they don't think that were an accident at all."

Käthchen Hückelhoven nodded portentously. "They thought she done herself in."

Scholten said: "What nonsense."

Grandmontagne said: "So you say. But they're bound to do it. If there's an accident, they got to think it could be different."

Quademichels stopped puffing his pipe. "Different like how?"

The Widow Abels waxed indignant. "Oh, shut your gob, Quademichels!"

Grandmontagne looked round. Then he said: "They got to think of murder, see? That's obvious, innit? And it's obvious who they suspect too. You can count the suspects on the fingers of one hand, Jupp."

"I can?" Scholten shook his head. "How would I know anything about it?"

Laudenberg said: "Well, take Wallmann. Who else?" He laughed. "He done well enough out of it, not half!"

Palm said: "You're a real pig, you are, Hubert."

"I'm what?"

"The man were shattered. S'pose your wife broke her neck, how'd you feel?"

Grandmontagne raised his voice. "It can't have been Wallmann. The cops say so. On account of my witness statement, understand? He got an alibi."

"You see?" said Palm.

Grandmontagne said: "He come in here while his wife's sitting at that table. And then he says he left something in the office, he's going back to fetch it. He were in a hurry. So he goes straight off and drives away. It couldn't've been him. He were on the road while Frau Wallmann was still sitting here alive and well."

Scholten said: "Yes, and then what?"

"Well, then she goes off too. She didn't stay around much longer. Yes, that were a bit odd, you ask Marlene. Am I right, Marlene?"

Frau Grandmontagne handed out the glasses and said: "Yes, that were odd." She wiped her hands on her apron and sat down on the edge of the corner seat. "She didn't say another word when Wallmann was gone. She suddenly jumps up like she's thought of something and off she goes. Nearly left the meat she'd bought behind."

Hückelhoven said: "Could've been going anywhere."

Käthchen Hückelhoven said: "We know where she were going. Up to the house and then she falls off the steps. Or maybe she don't."

Karl-Heinz Palm raised his glass and drank to Grandmontagne, who had bought this round.

Grandmontagne said: "And to poor Frau Wallmann. God rest her soul."

They drank, and for a moment there was silence. Then Quademichels said: "So what did the cops want with you, Granmontansch?"

The women screeched with laughter, Laudenberg kept slapping his thigh, Karl-Heinz Palm clapped the startled Quademichels on the shoulder. Hückelhoven ordered another round and an extra schnapps for Quademichels to get him over the shock. Scholten bought a round of schnapps for everyone after that, Palm was not to be outdone, and after the round of schnapps Palm had bought, Laudenberg bought a round of beer. "Can't get that stuff down without a chaser." Karl-Heinz Palm asked his father if he could lend him ten marks till tomorrow morning and bought the next round.

At eleven Scholten was dancing with Käthchen Hückelhoven, the others were watching, Grandmontagne was beating time, clapping his hands and exclaiming: "Hey, Jupp's a real goer." Hückelhoven stood up and said "Time to be off", and when Laudenberg asked what the hurry was he said he had to get up again and be in the bakery in three hours' time. He said "Come on, Käthchen, let's go," but Käthchen Hückelhoven said "You go alone, you don't need me to help you snore", and Hückelhoven went without saying goodnight.

At eleven-thirty Grandmontagne had laid a bet with Quademichels to decide who bought the next round; the bet was that Quademichels couldn't pick up his, Grandmontagne's, wife and sit her down on the bar. "She's a hundred and eighty pounds live weight, you'll never do it!" "What d'you bet?" Quademichels cried, "What d'you bet?" and then he stood up and seized hold of Marlene Grandmontagne, who twisted in his arms, shrieking, as he put one arm around her behind and the other around her shoulders and picked her up, the veins swelling on his forehead. As he took the first tottering step towards the bar he farted loudly, Marlene struggled like a wild thing, and Quademichels fell to the floor with her. They picked him up, and

Quademichels shouted, "What d'you bet? What d'you bet?" and reached for Marlene again, but she was cross by now and was holding her backside defensively.

They put Quademichels back in his seat, and there was an argument because he said he had won the bet, but he was shouted down. Palm said if Quademichels let out another fart like that he'd buy another round, no need for Quademichels to pick Marlene up again, and Quademichels shouted "You lost that one, then!" and was raising his bottom from the seat already, hands clutching the table top, but Marlene Grandmontagne pushed him in the chest and said: "Behave yourself, you old pig!" The Widow Abels wiped her eyes and asked to be let out of the corner seat, she said she'd laughed so much she'd wet her knickers.

At twelve Grandmontagne shouted, "Time, everyone, please!" They made their way noisily out of the door. The village street echoed to the sound. Scholten was trying to get hold of the Widow Abels, but the Palms, father and son, who were going the same way as the widow, took her arms and staggered away with her. Grandmontagne stuffed the rump steak Scholten had asked for in his jacket pocket and said: "Drive carefully, Jupp, mind you don't jump no lights."

Scholten set off, engine roaring. He hooted as he drove past Käthchen Hückelhoven. Laudenberg was supporting her. She waved to Scholten. He avoided Quademichels, who was swaying about in the middle of the road. When Scholten turned off along the woodland track he went a little too far to the right on the soft ground, but it was all right, he didn't even touch the tree. He was in bed at twelve-thirty. The house was perfectly still. He fell asleep.

14

Scholten woke at a quarter past six. He had left the window open overnight, and now he smelled the fresh morning air. The sky was pale blue above the dark trees. Scholten lay in bed a little longer. He stretched, yawned, listened to the birds. Then he said: "Come on, get up, Jupp Scholten. This is crunch time."

He put bacon in the frying pan, broke three of the eggs he had brought with him over it, made coffee. When he had eaten his breakfast he went into the living room. He opened a cupboard, pulled out a couple of drawers. The temptation was strong. But he must make sure he got the mainsail on the line. Wallmann would ask about that first.

He climbed down to the landing stage. Morning sunlight lay warm on the steps. He went to the boat, opened the chest in the fo'c'sle, took out the sail sack, heaved it over his shoulder and carried it up the steps to the garage.

He began by clearing the garage. He cleared everything stacked in the corners and along the walls, everything round the workbench at the back and in front of the shelves, and put it outside the garage. When the concrete floor was bare he cleaned it. He connected up the garden hose, sprayed the floor and scrubbed it clean, going right into the corners. Then he hosed it down once again.

Next he opened the sail sack. He spread the sail out on the garage floor. It didn't quite fit in; he turned up the footrope, went all round the sail once more and pulled it out smooth. Then he hosed the sail down.

When he went to the house to rinse the bucket and add warm water to the detergent in it he stopped by the jumble of boards, tools, car tyres, strips of wood, buckets, crates and boxes that he had cleared out. Something had caught his eye as he did it; he couldn't remember what it was.

Oh yes, the strips of wood. Last year he had panelled the entrance hall with lengths of wooden strips; he had meant to panel the sidewall of the lavatory too, but time was short, and Wallmann had said he could do the lavatory later. He had put the remaining lengths of wood in the garage.

There were not as many as there had been last year. That was what he'd noticed.

Scholten wondered what Wallmann had done with the strips. Surely he hadn't burned them as firewood? Those wooden strips hadn't been cheap. But Wallmann was capable of anything. Perhaps he'd run out of firewood and had been too lazy to chop more.

Scholten shook his head and went into the bathroom with his bucket and the detergent. When he came out he stopped to look at the lengths of wood again. There'd been a good ten yards left, if not fifteen. After a while he shook his head and turned away.

It was a hard job getting the sail on the line. He had taken the ladder out to the grass in front of the house and stretched the line a good eight feet above the ground, between two trees. The sail was heavy as lead. He tied the headboard to one of the trees and then draped the sail over the line, half each side. Twice he very nearly slipped on the grass.

When he had finished the job he fetched himself a bottle of beer from the fridge. He cast a satisfied glance at his provisions. Before leaving town he had gone to the supermarket to buy half a crate of beer, a small bottle of schnapps and a bottle of wine.

He took his beer out of doors, put the bottle to his lips, drank half of it then looked at those wooden strips. He was going to sit down on the seat under the oak tree then turned back when he was halfway there and began counting the strips. He paused, said: "Hold on a moment, Jupp Scholten. Don't get confused. Stop and think how many there really were."

He looked up at the sky, frowned. It wasn't long before he remembered. Yes, there had been twenty-eight strips left, each seven feet long. That would have been enough for the side wall of the lavatory. The lavatory was seven feet high, just like the hall. Scholten had ordered the strips cut to size.

There had been exactly twenty-eight strips measuring seven feet left over last year. And one remnant about twenty inches long. Scholten had had to piece bits of the wooden strips together over the doors and round the electricity meter in the hall.

The remnant was here. Scholten counted the seven-foot strips. There were twenty-three.

Five strips missing.

Abstractedly he went back into the house, stopped in the hall. He glanced into the lavatory. Then he searched the whole house for anywhere Wallmann could have fitted the strips. Nothing. Those five wooden strips had disappeared.

He went out of the house again. He wondered whether he could allow himself a second bottle of beer before he went back to work. The area in front of the house looked a mess with all the stuff lying about there.

Suddenly he stood very still. He stayed like that for a

while, and then went into the garage. He was looking for the folding rule; he swept the spanners and pliers on the workbench carelessly aside. He found the rule, took it out of the garage and down to the steps. He kneeled on the landing and measured the two steps just above it. Then he measured the three planks of the landing itself.

He didn't really need to; he knew the measurements of the steps from last year when he had replaced the old, weather-worn planks. But he wanted to make sure.

It was exactly right. Each plank was about twenty-eight inches broad and nine and a half inches deep.

Scholten sat down on the landing of the steps and began calculating, his lips moving silently. The five planks with greased bolts had a total length along their long and short sides of ten times twenty-eight and ten times nine and a half inches. That made twenty-three feet four inches and seven feet eleven inches. In all, thirty-one feet three inches.

The five missing strips were more than eleven yards long in all. Roughly the length of all the sides of those planks put together.

There was a remnant left, of course. When Wallmann cut up the strips to nail them round the edges of the planks, he was bound to have pieces left over. For instance, he could cut a strip measuring seven feet into three pieces of twenty-eight inches each, but after cutting strips for the ends there would still be a small remnant that he couldn't use.

Scholten stared out at the lake. He was sure he was on the right track. The fresh grease on the bolts in the five planks couldn't be coincidence. Or the fact that these were the planks where a fall could be dangerous. Or that there were nail-holes on all four sides of those planks. Or that several strips had disappeared without

110

trace. Or that these strips amounted in all to about the same length as the sides of the five planks added together.

But why? Why had he nailed a frame of strips round the planks? And then taken the strips away again and fitted the planks back in place? It was nonsense.

Scholten struck his forehead with his fist. "Hell, it must make sense somehow! Think, Jupp Scholten. What's your brain-box for?" He stared at the distant bank on the far side of the lake. Suddenly he looked at his watch. "Shit." It was nearly one o'clock. The sun was already behind the house.

He went up to the kitchen, chopped an onion, browned it and tipped the can of mushrooms he had brought with him into the pan. He drank two bottles of beer with his lunch. Then he went out and got down to work.

He had already moved some of the junk from outside the house back into the garage when he stopped. "You're crazy!" he told himself. "This is where you must look, Jupp Scholten, here. And if you don't find anything here then you can always look in the house."

He began with the workbench. He cleared it and the shelves. He looked at everything he picked up.

After a quarter of an hour he had found a tin containing bolts. They were the same size as the bolts fixing the planks of the steps in place. When he replaced the six planks last autumn he hadn't used new bolts for them all. There were a few left over.

But there were more here than those he had left. And most of them were quite new and freshly greased. He counted ten bolts with traces of that fresh grease.

Scholten looked at the bolts for a while. He turned them this way and that. He thought hard. And light suddenly dawned.

He went out and looked for the old planks, the ones he had replaced. Last autumn he had left them in a corner of the garage, and when he cleared it out this morning he had put them aside. He examined them one by one. It was very difficult to make out, but finally he was more or less sure that there were traces of fresh grease in some of the holes in the planks through which the bolts had passed.

It seemed to him perfectly clear why those traces were there: Wallmann had thought the chance that someone might notice the hole in the flight of steps too much of a risk. So he had replaced the five planks he had taken out with five of the old planks, just until he could refit the others. And he had greased the bolts so that the whole process could be carried out quickly and easily.

Scholten thought for a while, but the point of this operation still eluded him. "Just take it easy," he whispered to himself. "We'll find out!"

He went on clearing the stuff up, taking the rest of the things back into the garage, inspecting everything. It was over an hour before he made another find. But then he had a strong feeling that he was getting very close to the solution of the puzzle.

Among the last items he put away in the garage were a couple of cardboard cartons, and in one of them Scholten found two rolls of the thick insulating tape he had used in the autumn to draught-proof the windows and door of the house. He had started one roll, but the other had still been complete.

Scholten was about to put the rolls away when he realized that both had been broken into. This time he didn't have to think for very long. He picked up the folding rule and measured the rolls. Four and a half yards were gone from one. That must be the one he had used himself.

A good ten yards were missing from the other.

Scholten smiled grimly and nodded.

Yes, of course, if you were going to put insulating tape round all the sides of those five planks then you'd need about ten yards.

But the triumph he felt did not last very long. This idea fitted too. It all fitted: the length of the planks, the length of the wooden strips and the insulating tape, the nail-marks. However, basically this was getting more and more complicated.

Everything indicated that Wallmann had taken the planks, put insulating tape round them, nailed the strips on them and then removed the strips and the insulating tape again, and refitted the planks in the flight of steps. But why do all this?

The whole thing was looking more and more nonsensical.

Just a moment, Jupp Scholten! Let's begin again at the beginning!

Hardly noticing what he was doing, he put his car in the garage, closed the garage door, went into the house, took a bottle of beer out of the fridge, went out again and sat down on the seat outside the house. He looked at the bottle, but he did not drink.

Take it easy, Jupp Scholten! What *is* your brain-box for? Go on, use it. Take it very easy.

Why had Wallmann worked on the steps?

Obvious: he had done something to make Erika fall. He had fixed things so that she'd be bound to think she could catch him down on the landing stage with his bit of fluff. And then he had set a trap on the steps and driven off to make sure of his alibi.

Right. What kind of a trap?

It had to have been a trap that no one could notice next morning, or the risk would have been too great.

He had gone to the bowling club on Friday evening and got so drunk, probably on purpose, that he couldn't drive back to the house until the following afternoon. Yes, of course he did it on purpose, because that gave him his bomb-proof alibi.

But it could have been very dangerous if the trap were something visible. He could have removed all traces after his return to the house, of course. He'd have had enough time, even if the local cop came at once. But before his return, before late Saturday afternoon, anyone could have passed the house or gone up the steps and might have seen the trap.

It had to be a trap that would leave no traces of itself. But did such a thing exist?

Just a moment! Let's take this one thing at a time.

The idea of the stretched cords. It would have worked. He'd thought it out. Didn't make sense all the same. Much too risky. Anyone could have found the cords.

The idea of the soft soap. That had sounded good too at first. How had he thought it up? That's right: he was wondering how Wallmann could have made the steps slippery. But again, the risk would have been far too great. Wallmann couldn't have scrubbed the soft soap off the steps until Saturday evening. And a lot could happen by then. No, that was no good either.

Scholten rubbed his forehead. Yes, and after the soft soap he'd had the idea about the ice. Again it wouldn't work. Or so Frings said anyway. And he was probably right. Impossible. How *would* you make ice form on the steps up to the cathedral? Rubbish, couldn't be done.

Suddenly Scholten held his breath. He raised a hand to his mouth very slowly and laid it on his lips.

A memory had suddenly intruded into his attempts to think logically and check everything off point by point. It hit him like a blow, heat ran through him, he felt his heart beating hard and fast.

He saw himself standing in the phone box, listening to the voice of the journalist Frings. "You'd need, as it were, to build a huge fridge over the road or round the cathedral steps. But that would surely be rather expensive, don't you think, Herr Höffner?"

Scholten began to smile. He looked at the house without really seeing it. His smile grew broader and broader.

He said: "Oh yes? You really think so, Herr Frings? Impossible, you say, Herr Frings? Well, you listen to me, clever Herr Frings. Who says you'd have to build a fridge over the steps? What about just putting the steps in the fridge? How about that, Herr Frings?"

He suddenly stood up. He realized that he was still holding the full beer bottle. He put the bottle carefully down on the seat, went to the garage, pushed the door up and went to the freezer. He opened the lid and looked in.

It was a chest freezer, only half full. He looked at the shelf above it. There were the two big coolbags that Wallmann took out in the boat with him in summer. The food in the freezer would easily fit into the two bags.

And the freezer was big enough to take more than five planks.

Scholten closed the lid of the freezer and leaned both arms on it. He nodded. He gave a grim smile. He had found the answer. He was on the bastard's trail. Wallmann, you've overplayed your hand.

He closed the garage door, went back to the seat. He sat down beside the beer bottle, but still he did not drink. He kept on nodding.

Yes, it was perfectly simple. He had the answer.

15

That was how it had been. That was how it must have been. Wallmann had come back to the house earlier. Indeed, on Thursday night. He had moored the boat near the fisherman's hut on Thursday evening to spend the night there. Laudenberg had seen him: that was evidence. Wallmann had gone into the fisherman's hut in the evening, maybe had something to eat, had something to drink anyway. And he hadn't taken anyone there, no, not that evening. He'd been alone on his boat, apparently to sleep the night in it.

But during the night he had secretly left the boat. He had gone to the house on foot, through the woods. He could do it in just under an hour.

He had taken out the five planks and fitted five of the old ones instead. He had taken the planks he'd removed into the garage, along with their bolts. He had cut the strips to size.

And then he had stuck the thick insulating tape on the edges of the planks. And he had nailed the boards over it. He'd nailed them so that they came about an inch and a half above the top surface of the planks. And yes, he had plenty of material available: he had cut the strips for the narrow sides a little longer, making them overlap on both sides so that the structure would hold and the frame he had made around the plank was firmly closed.

The result would be a set of small basins, rectangular wooden bowls. Each plank had a frame round it, waterproofed with insulating tape and coming about an inch and a half above the plank itself. He had filled those wooden bowls with water to a depth of an inch or so. And he had put them in the freezer. Yes, and he'd left the bolts in the planks, or he wouldn't have been able to screw them in again later when the water on top of the planks had frozen to ice.

He also needed the bolts to block up the holes bored in the planks. He had screwed the nuts on so tightly that the heads of the bolts closed the holes.

The shanks of the bolts stood out underneath the planks, but that was no problem. He had stood the first plank – the first bowl he placed in the freezer – on two blocks of wood, or maybe a shallow box. And then he had put the next bowls on top of the first one, each crossing the one below at an angle to leave room for the shanks of the bolts.

Perhaps a little water had trickled through the places where two strips of insulating tape met or through the holes made for the bolts, but if he had turned the freezer to fast-freeze the water would be frozen before it ran out.

In the end each plank was covered with a sheet of ice. The sheet had to be smooth as glass.

Black ice

Black ice made in the freezer.

Scholten ran one hand through his hair and pinched his cheeks with the other.

And Wallmann could even have made his sheets of black ice slope. If he tilted the bowls slightly in the freezer, with a piece of wood placed under them, they would have stood at a slight angle. And the water would have come a little higher one side of the plank than the other. So when the water froze to ice it would have sloped.

He could have fixed it, with those bowls, so that the black ice on the landing and the two steps above it sloped down. How could Erika have kept her footing then? She had no chance when she started down the steps, suspecting nothing.

Scholten gritted his teeth and clenched his fists.

Slowly. Take it easy. One thing after another. Think it out right to the end.

That bloody bastard. He'd put his bowls, his little rectangular basins of water in the freezer, and then he'd set it to fast-freeze. It would take a lot of electricity, but that didn't matter. He'd cleared everything away, and then he'd gone back through the wood to the fisherman's hut. He had gone to sleep in his bunk in the boat. Everything was ready, in perfect order.

And next day he had probably damaged the tackle of the mainsheet himself. A couple of blows with a hammer would make it stick. He had gone into the yachting basin and then played his little game with the phone at three o'clock and five o'clock on Friday afternoon. He wanted Erika to think something was up. Something wrong. And at five he was back at the house, he'd just wanted to make sure Erika was still in town and he had enough time in hand.

He had waited until the sun set and it was getting cold again. He had lit a fire on the hearth. Erika liked a fire on the hearth.

And then he had gone down to the steps and removed the old planks again. He had put them away in the garage and taken his black ice planks out of the freezer. He'd knocked away the wooden strips, torn off the insulating tape, that wouldn't take long. He had carried the icy planks down and fitted them on the steps.

And then he had gone up to the garage and put the

bolts of the substitute planks away in the tin, and he had taken the wooden strips and the remains of the insulating tape into the house and thrown them on the fire. He had looked around once more, yes, nothing forgotten, everything in order, and then he had got into his car and driven to Grandmontagne's. Erika was sitting there with her grog, he'd said he had to drive back to town for those files, and then he'd gone off and fixed his alibi.

That bloody bastard. It really was a perfect alibi. Because next morning the sun would have shone full on the steps as soon as it rose over the eastern bank of the lake. And probably the last of the ice would have melted by midday. The planks might still be slightly dark from the moisture, but even that last trace would have faded by the afternoon.

And if the plan hadn't worked, if Erika hadn't gone down the steps, even then he had nothing to fear. Because in that case too the ice would have melted, and the trap would probably never have been discovered.

The bastard! An idea just waiting to be thought up. Black ice. Melting and leaving no trace.

But he'd miscalculated. Jupp Scholten had found him out. Jupp Scholten had used his brain-box and found him out.

Scholten abruptly reached for the bottle, put it to his lips, drank the entire contents, belched loudly. He stood up, stretched his arms. Then he took aim and flung the bottle far into the wood. He called, "You watch out, Wallmann! The game's up!"

He pushed up the garage door, put his bucket away and took down the shutters over the windows.

He finished at six-thirty. He had washed and sand-papered the shutters, had filled in a few notches here and there. He could be finished by tomorrow afternoon. He'd even have time to do something about the weeds.

He went into the house and took the chips out of the frozen food compartment of the fridge. Then he went into the garage.

He put one of the old planks on the workbench and stuck the thick insulating tape around its edges. He took one of the wooden strips and cut four pieces off it with the circular saw, two of them measuring twenty-eight inches and the others measuring twelve.

He nailed the strips to the edges of the plank. He let the shorter strips overlap on both sides, and he used four nails for each of the longer strips and two for each of the shorter ones. He made sure the nails went through the insulating tape.

He nailed the strips in place so that they were about an inch above the upper surface of the plank, setting only one of the shorter strips rather lower. He bent down, so that his eyes were level with the workbench, and examined the basin he had made from the plank. It stood at a slight angle.

He put the bolts in the holes in the plank and tightened the nuts. He placed the contents of the freezer in the two coolbags. Then he filled his little basin with water to a level of about three-quarters of an inch. He put it carefully in the freezer and closed the lid, setting it to fast-freeze.

He closed the garage door, went to the bathroom and washed. Then he went into the kitchen. He washed the lettuce, dressed it, put the chips on to fry. He put the rump steak in the pan at seven-thirty.

After his meal he took his beer bottle outside. Darkness was coming up from the woods. The birds had fallen silent. He walked round the house, gravel crunching under his shoes. The windows were bright, sharply outlined like the yellowish-red slits in a large black Chinese lantern. He went to the steps leading down to the steep bank and sat on the top step.

The lake was calm. Now and then a ripple lapped against the boat, and the landing stage creaked slightly.

Scholten said: "Just wait, Erika. He's overplayed his hand! I promised you." After a while he took out his handkerchief and wiped his eyes. He put the handkerchief away and stared at the landing on the steps, which could hardly be made out in the twilight.

Scholten shivered. He rose and went indoors. He switched on the TV and sat in an armchair for a while, watching in silence, drinking his beer. Suddenly he picked up the phone book and looked for the name of the Widow Abels. Lisbeth. He ran his finger over the pages. Abels, Lisbeth, that must be her.

He rubbed his chin. Then he dialled the number.

No one answered.

He hung up, went into the kitchen and took his bottle of wine out of the fridge.

16

Scholten spent all weekend wondering how best to inform the police about the murder. It wasn't as simple as he had thought at first.

He was absolutely sure that Wallmann had murdered Erika. His experiment had provided the final proof. For it had worked. When he had taken his rectangular basin out of the freezer early on Friday morning there was a smooth solid layer of ice on the plank. He had knocked away the strips, torn off the insulating tape, and burned it all in the fire on the hearth. He had placed the ice-covered plank out behind the garage in the morning sun. In the afternoon the layer of ice had disappeared from the plank, the water had trickled away into the gravel, the wood was beginning to dry out.

There was no doubt about the method Wallmann had used to murder Erika.

But how could he convince the police of it?

At first he intended to go to the police station on Saturday morning, ask to see the head of the murder squad and tell him the whole story. But he very soon had misgivings about this idea.

He didn't know whether the head of the murder squad would be at work on Saturday. He tried to think whether he'd ever seen a crime film on TV where the superintendent or the featured detective had been in the office on a Saturday, but he really couldn't remember. Of course, if a body was found somewhere they went out to the crime scene even on a Saturday or Sunday. This often happened to Felmy in the TV detective series, because he'd be with his ex-wife at weekends, trying to get together with her again.

But Scholten did not think the head of the murder squad would be sitting in his office on a Saturday just in case he had visitors. High-ranking police officers wanted their weekends off too. And there was no point talking to just any stupid police constable. In fact it could be a big mistake. Because the police constable would at the very least want to know his name, and then they might call Hilde on Monday. Or they might call the works and ask for information. And then he'd be in trouble.

No. He must go to the police station on a normal working day. Preferably in the morning when he'd be able to speak to the boss. At eight or nine, maybe. Not too early. They always have conferences first thing, he'd often seen them do that on TV.

But even so it wasn't easy. He'd have to find some kind of excuse to leave the works.

Or to arrive late. It would take him at least an hour to explain everything to the superintendent. Call it two hours with the drive there and back. And if he went straight to the police station from home and was there by nine, he couldn't be at the works before ten-thirty. So he'd be arriving a whole four hours late at the office.

He couldn't really say he had diarrhoea again.

He put off the decision all week. On Friday morning he decided to think it over thoroughly again at the weekend. For by now he had realized that even a conversation with the head of the murder squad could be horribly risky.

What evidence could he offer the police? Damned little. The nail-marks. The grease on the bolts. That was about it. And the new bolts that hadn't been in the tin before. But how was he to prove how many bolts had been there in the first place? And how many strips of wood, and how much insulating tape?

The wood had disappeared, gone up the chimney in smoke. So had the insulating tape. And as for the black ice, well, that was the point: the main piece of evidence had melted away the day after the murder, leaving no trace.

And what would happen if they really did investigate: followed up his information and interrogated Wallmann? Wallmann would simply claim: "Scholten is crazy. He's afraid I'll sack him. And he's right too, he's useless. He wants to save his own bacon by pinning something on me. What he says is pure nonsense. No such thing happened. Prove it."

And suppose the proof wasn't strong enough? Or the police were too stupid to prosecute Wallmann? Then what?

He could answer that question at once. Then he'd be out of his job in the office of Ferd. Köttgen, Civil Engineering Contractors. He'd be on the dole until he reached retirement age.

And Wallmann would be finally off the hook. A dreadful prospect. It simply must not happen. Jupp Scholten wasn't resigning himself to that. There had to be a way.

He thought and thought, but he kept going round in circles.

At some point in the following week, on his way home, he became engrossed in the idea of proving it to the police himself. He could show them how you made a rectangular basin like that, and how easy it was to cover the planks of the steps with black ice. Then they'd have to believe him.

But as he was sitting in front of the TV screen he suddenly shook his head vigorously. You must have had too much to drink, Jupp Scholten! You'd only find yourself deeper in the shit.

It was far too risky to tell the police he'd tried it out and it worked. That might put other ideas into their heads. "Tell us, Herr Scholten, could you perhaps have been planning a little accident yourself? Intended for your own wife, maybe? Herr Wallmann offered to let you take your wife to his weekend retreat with you, isn't that right? Could it be that now you've taken fright and thought better of it, and you've thought of pinning something on your boss? You don't get on too well with Herr Wallmann, do you, Herr Scholten? Hasn't he already threatened to sack you?"

The mere idea made him feel hot under the collar. He shifted restlessly in his armchair. He realized they could simply say he himself was responsible for the nail-holes in the planks. And the grease. They could say he'd been rehearsing the whole thing, not with just one of the substitute planks but with the five from the steps.

Hilde said: "Can't you sit still? How can I concentrate on the film? I wish I knew why you have to keep shifting about."

He said in a very loud voice: "Because I want to!" and then stood up and went into the kitchen. As he was opening the bottle of beer she appeared in the doorway. She said in a penetrating whisper: "Do you have to shout like that? What's the matter with you?"

He raised the bottle to his lips and drank.

"You act in such a common way!" she whispered.

He put the bottle down, belched and said: "I *am* common."

Her voice turning reedy, she said: "Yes, I knew that

from the start. I should never have married you. I'd have saved myself a lot of grief. If I hadn't married you I might still be healthy. But of course it didn't matter to you whether I was strong enough to have children."

He belched again copiously.

She sobbed and went away.

Until the next weekend, he kept wondering whether he could do it anonymously. It couldn't be done over the phone. That was much too complicated: he could never explain what it was all about in two or three sentences. If he did it anonymously he would have to write a letter.

He knew from the first that a letter was even more dangerous than a phone call. They would get on his trail; they investigate such letters. But he thought up dozens of ways of writing that letter. He realized how difficult it was to describe the trap, but he kept trying. He did not actually put anything down on paper: too risky. Someone might have come along and asked what he was writing. And he kept finding himself assailed by a torrent of fragmentary ideas that he couldn't control.

He spent the weekend brooding.

On Monday afternoon the door of the filing room was suddenly flung open. Wallmann marched in, shouting: "How much longer do I have to wait for those bank statements? I said I needed them at once!"

Scholten, who had started in surprise, realized that Wallmann was addressing not him but Rosa Thelen. Rosie instantly burst into tears. You could hardly make anything of the shrill broken sounds she uttered between her sobs. "But – but you wanted – you wanted – the statements from the – the job centre – you wanted them at once – too – "

Wallmann roared: "Yes? So what? Is that too much to

ask? I thought you were supposed to be a book-keeper?"

"But – but I can – "

"I know just what you can do. You can sit on your fat arse and twiddle your thumbs. And make coffee. You can't do anything else. I'm sick of it. Things are going to change around here, you bet your life they are!"

Rosie was weeping bitterly. Wallmann went out, slamming the door. Scholten, who had been looking at some papers with his head bowed, looked up and said: "The bastard. I'll pay him back, I promise you I will. Stop crying, Rosie. He can't do anything to you."

Rosa Thelen went on crying and looking through the bank statements at top speed, meanwhile wiping the corners of her eyes with her wrist.

On the way home Scholten turned into a side street. After driving round a couple of corners he found a phone box in a fairly quiet street. He got out of the car, gritting his teeth, went into the phone box, found the number of the police station in the phone book. He took out his handkerchief, as if to blow his nose, raised the receiver to his ear with his other hand. Just as he realized that he hadn't looked round outside the phone box, a woman's voice answered. "Police here."

He almost dropped the handkerchief and with trembling fingers tried to drape part of it over the receiver without removing it from his nose.

"Hello? Police here."

Scholten said: "Frau Erika Wallmann, of the civil engineering firm of Ferdinand Köttgen, she didn't die in an accident. She was murdered. By her husband. You should investigate . . ." Then he broke off, hesitated, hung the receiver up in a moment of sudden panic. He pushed open the door of the phone box, almost colliding with an old lady walking down the road with her shopping bag. He turned his face away, got into his car, drove off with the engine roaring. He thought that, in the rear-view mirror, he saw the old lady looking after him.

17

When he got home it occurred to him that he hadn't tried to disguise his voice. He stood beside his car, briefcase in hand, both arms dangling. "Oh, shit," he said.

Nothing happened for the next few days. The following week passed without any incident too. Scholten began to feel calmer. If they had recorded his voice on tape they'd have turned up at the works some time or other. After all, he had given the name of the firm. They'd have come and played everyone the tape and asked: "Do you know this voice?"

Perhaps they might yet turn up?

For they should at least have come to question Wallmann. This was a murder case when all was said and done.

Perhaps they'd summoned Wallmann to the police station? Or perhaps they had gone to his apartment. In the evening. Two of them. They'd stood outside the front door, and when he opened it they'd shown their ID and said: "CID. May we speak to you for a moment, Herr Wallmann?" They had gone into the living room with him and stood there in their raincoats, looking around them.

It gave Scholten a fright to think that they might have played Wallmann their tape. "What do you have to say about this, Herr Wallmann? You'll understand that we have to investigate the matter. Have you any idea who the man could be?"

It took him some time to calm down again. No, surely that was out of the question. If they'd played Wallmann the tape, the wheels would have started going round by now.

No, there was only one possibility: they were quietly investigating for themselves. They were doing the only right thing. They weren't interested in the man who made the call. They were interested in the murderer. Perhaps they were already closing in on Wallmann. Some time or other they'd be coming to take him away.

Scholten nurtured this hope all through June, and he was still living on it when July came. Sometimes it gave him a pang to see the murderer walking around, still a free man. And whenever Wallmann raised his voice in anger at the works Scholten clenched his fist in the pocket of his overall and said to himself: "You wait, you bastard! I'm sick of this! You're for the chop!"

But when his initial alarm and his anger had worn off, he always found himself back exactly where he had been before. What could he do?

He'd already done everything he could. It was up to the police now. They knew what had happened, damn it! Why were they taking so long about it? Why didn't they do anything?

In August Scholten went on holiday with Hilde for three weeks. They spent the first two weeks in a little boarding house not far from the Baltic coast, as they did every year. Scholten went fishing. Hilde lay in a lounger on the balcony recovering from the stress of the journey.

She had few objections to fishing. Many years ago she had decided that fishing was a healthy sport, unlike the bowling that Scholten had previously said was the kind of sport that suited him and kept him fit.

Hilde liked to eat fish too because of its high protein content. Protein is good for the nerves.

Hilde spent her days in the second week recovering from the noise young people on holiday made in the street at night. Scholten didn't hear them. He didn't wake up at night except when Hilde nudged him and asked if he couldn't hear all that noise.

In the middle of the second week Hilde said Scholten was overdoing his fishing. Overdoing anything was always a bad idea, even overdoing an activity that was healthy in itself. Couldn't he take an interest in something else? He might read a book for once.

So Scholten stayed at the boarding house for a day, leafing through the biography of Pope John Paul II that Hilde had brought with her. In the afternoon he went down to the tobacconist and bought a thriller, Hubert Steinbecker's *Deadly Bait*. The book disappointed him. It had nothing at all to do with fishing. Hilde had disapproved of its purchase anyway.

And as they did every year, they spent the third week visiting Angelika in Kiel. Scholten taught his grandson to play skat. The boy was a quick learner, and after Scholten had taught him the rules they played every day. Hilde tried to stop the games, but Scholten said they would help the boy to learn to multiply in his head and do it fast. Angelika said that would certainly be good for her son. Scholten's son-in-law, a pharmacist by profession, had no objection. He knew nothing about card games. Hilde was not at all happy.

On the way home Scholten wanted to leave the motorway at Blumenthal. He said it would be only a little longer to go by way of the Brahmsee, and maybe they could catch a glimpse of the Chancellor's holiday home, maybe Helmut Schmidt himself would be out sailing on the lake, he'd always been interested in sailing. Hilde said this was all she needed, she didn't know how she was going to stand the drive back anyway: she was feeling very unwell.

Scholten passed the exit road to Blumenthal. He was driving very fast. Hilde asked why he had to rush along like that; it made her feel dizzy. And the cat didn't like it either, the cat would go frantic again. Scholten said the cat didn't mind at all. He put his arm behind him, patted the cat basket and said: "Isn't that right, Manny?" The cat mewed. "There you are," said Scholten.

He abandoned himself to a daydream for the rest of the journey. He returned to his daydream after every interruption by Hilde, he imagined it all in detail.

He saw himself going to the works on Monday morning, they were all there already, strangely enough, even Kurowski. All but Wallmann. They were standing in the project managers' office. He asked: "What's up?" Büttgenbach looked at him and said: "Haven't you heard? Herr Wallmann's been arrested." Inge Faust was crying.

When Scholten went to the works on Monday morning Wallmann was out in the yard with the chief mechanic, inspecting the surface finisher that had been overhauled at the weekend. Standing high up on the surface finisher, he looked down and said: "Had a good time?"

"Yes thanks, very good."

"And how's your wife?"

Scholten realized that he had put his hope in the police in vain. They hadn't taken his phone call seriously. Perhaps they hadn't understood it. There hadn't even been a policeman at the other end of the line, only that stupid female. He'd probably interrupted her in the middle of painting her nails. Very likely she hadn't even passed the message on.

Over the next few days Scholten tried to think of another approach. But none of his ideas came to anything. He knew in advance that he would always reach a point where the whole thing could be dangerous to himself. Very dangerous.

In addition, Wallmann was behaving reasonably well. This went on for some time. Plenty of orders were coming in. One afternoon in September, when Scholten had found him a few files, Wallmann even offered him the cigar box. "Like one?"

Scholten said "If I may," and selected a cigar.

Wallmann said: "Herr Scholten, we have a bit of leeway, but the boat will have to be prepared for winter quarters some time. You know what to do, dismantling all the gear and so on. Could you maybe drive over next month and see to it? I should think a day would be enough."

Scholten turned the cigar in his fingers. "And all those weeds will need to come out too. They grow like nobody's business up there."

"I don't mind if you stay there two days. I'll pay you."

"Yes, well, I must just see how I can fix it with my wife."

"Take her with you, why don't you?"

"Well, I'll think about that." Drive to the lake with Hilde. That was all he needed!

When he left Wallmann's office his conscience smote him. He looked at the cigar with distaste, put it down on his desk. He went over to the window, looked up at the sky and said in his mind: "Erika, help me. Why don't you tell me what to do?"

Fifteen minutes later he lit the cigar again. It

wouldn't do Erika any good for him to throw the expensive thing away.

In mid-September heavy rain set in. A couple of building sites were flooded. The mood in the office was low. Büttgenbach was away for four weeks, having a kidney stone operation. The weather improved but not the mood in the office.

Early one afternoon Wallmann came striding out of his office. He shouted down the corridor: "Kurowski, come here at once. The sewer in Adenauerstrasse has collapsed."

"What?" cried Kurowski in alarm. "How did that happen?"

Wallmann stood there in the doorway, bellowing. "Didn't you hear? Rothgerber called – there's someone underneath it! That bastard Vierkotten, he didn't shore it up!"

Kurowski came out with his overcoat in his hand. Scholten ran after them, calling: "Shall I come too?" Wallmann got into his car, slammed the door, opened it again and shouted: "No, you stay here, what would you do on the site, just stand there, staring?" Scholten went in again. He told Rosie and Inge Faust what had happened. Half an hour later the phone rang. Scholten answered it.

It was a reporter from the newspaper. He wanted to know about the accident in Adenauerstrasse.

Scholten said: "Well, these things do sometimes happen, you know. After this rain. And probably the foreman of the excavation crew didn't realize that they'd taken the sewer down too deep."

The reporter asked the foreman's name.

"Vierkotten," said Scholten. "Matthias Vierkotten."

The reporter asked what he meant about taking the sewer too deep.

134

Scholten said: "Well, it's like this, you see, when you're digging a tunnel for a sewer, and it gets to four feet deep or more, you have to shore it up. Support it with boards on both sides, left and right. So the earth doesn't collapse in on it, do you see?"

The reporter said yes, he saw, and did that mean the sewer in Adenauerstrasse hadn't been shored up?

Scholten began to feel slightly uncomfortable. He said: "Well, I don't really know. I haven't been to the site myself. We're all waiting to find out what happened."

The reporter said he supposed it was against regulations not to shore it up.

Scholten repeated: "We're all waiting to find out what happened."

The reporter asked if he could tell him his name.

"Oh, that's of no importance," said Scholten. "Just say the firm of Ferdinand Köttgen, Civil Engineering Contractors. The Ferdinand's abbreviated. F-e-r-d, full stop."

The reporter said he really did need his name. Was he one of the company executives?

Scholten said: "Yes, but there's no need to write that. And like I said, we're all still waiting to find out what happened. Goodbye." And he hung up.

Rosa looked at him. She said: "Didn't you tell him a bit too much?"

Scholten said: "Oh, what the hell."

But he still felt uncomfortable.

18

Next morning Wallmann called everyone into his office. He was sitting at his desk, both arms resting on it. The newspaper lay in front of him. When they were all there Wallmann looked up and said: "Who told the newspaper fellow this stuff?"

No one said anything.

Wallmann said: "I have my own strong suspicions." He looked at Scholten.

Scholten said: "Why are you looking at me like that?"

"Because it was you who talked to the newspaper fellow."

"What makes you say so? What's in the paper anyway?"

"Don't pretend you haven't already read it. No piece of paper is safe from you."

Scholten said: "I won't be spoken to like that."

"And don't answer back." Wallmann smoothed out the newspaper, leaned over it and read: "According to the Civil Engineering Inspectorate, a tunnel of four feet in depth must be shored up, that is to say, the sides must be supported by wooden planks or iron plates. A company executive at Köttgen admitted as much. The tunnel for the sewer in Adenauerstrasse was nearly five feet deep but had not been shored up. One of the staff at the Civil Engineering Inspectorate added that the recklessness with which some firms tried to save on labour costs was astonishing. Such cases are only too often forgotten when commissions for public works are allotted."

Wallmann leaned back and looked at Scholten.

Rothgerber said: "He got it from the Civil Engineering Inspectorate obviously. Could have been that bastard Fassbender."

Kurowski said: "That's right, ever since Herr Rothgerber had that little spat with Fassbender he's had it in for us."

"And how about this company executive of Köttgen?" Wallmann brought the flat of his hand down on the newspaper. "Just who can he have been? We were all on the building site." He jerked his chin at Rothgerber. "You sent one reporter packing yourself." He looked at Scholten again. "No one was here but Herr Scholten. Herr Scholten the executive."

Scholten said: "I won't be spoken to like that."

"You'll be spoken to however I please, understand?" Wallmann leaned forward, half lowering his head, and looked at Scholten from under his brows. "Let's get this quite clear, Mister Executive, it looks like you've been lucky again. I called the newspaper. That fellow answered back too. Said he didn't have to tell me the name of his informant. Could be he's right, I'm not sure. I'll ask my lawyer. So maybe you really are in luck, Scholten. Yet again. But you mark my words: one more incident like that and you're out on your ear. I'll be sacking you for damage to the company's interests. And don't start thinking I won't get it past the industrial tribunal."

Rothgerber stood up and said: "Is that all?"

"Yes, that's all. I wasn't intending to keep you from your work any longer. Get ready, would you, Rothgerber? The man from the industrial insurance association is coming at eleven."

Out in the corridor, Rothgerber said: "You must be out of your mind, giving a reporter a story like that."

Scholten said: "What do you mean?" His heart was thudding in his throat.

Kurowski said: "Oh, never mind. It would all have come out anyway."

Rosa was already at her desk. She didn't look up. Scholten sat down, looked through his papers for a while. Then he said: "Talk about high and mighty! And he tells the foremen himself they don't have to shore up every last little piss-hole."

Rosa said, without looking up, "But he can sack you."

"Him? He's going to get a big surprise."

"You can't do anything to him."

"That's what you think. That's what you think, Rosie." He leaned forward and sang, "Oh, oh, oh, if you did but know all . . ."

Rosa shook her head decidedly, pushed her chair back and went out.

That afternoon Scholten had trouble with one of the Yugoslavians. The man had come into the office and was about to drive away in his big, battered car when Scholten saw him through the window. Scholten leaped to his feet, stood in the doorway of the office building and whistled through his fingers. He waved. "Hey, you!"

The Yugoslav stopped, wound down his window. "Me?"

"Yes, you. Come over here."

The Yugoslav hesitated then reluctantly got out and came over to Scholten.

"What's your name?"

"Me?"

"Yes, you, who else?"

The Yugoslav stroked his moustache and then said: "Herr Protic. Milan Protic."

"Right, Milan. Here." Scholten held out a packet that he had done up after seeing the Yugoslav arrive. "You can give that to your foreman."

Protic looked at the packet. "What is it?"

"That's nothing to do with you. It's private."

Protic said: "Then take it yourself. I not postman." He turned and went back to his car, saying not loudly, but very clearly: "Arsehole."

Scholten shouted: "You watch out, my friend, or I'll show you who's the arsehole around here!" He nodded vigorously and at length. The Yugoslav spat and drove away.

That evening, when Scholten was climbing the stairs, old Frau Kannegiesser opened the door of her apartment and said: "Herr Scholten, that business with your cat, it can't go on."

"What can't go on?"

"The way you keep letting it up and down past my balcony."

"What bothers you about it?"

"I always get such a fright when the creature comes down. There I am on my balcony and down comes the cat. It could jump on my head. It's a nasty animal."

"It's not half as nasty as you." Scholten went on climbing the stairs.

"That's outrageous! I'll complain to the cooperative, you toad, you drunk!"

"Oh, for goodness' sake, go boil . . ." But Scholten bit back the rest of what he had been about to say.

Hilde was waiting for him with the door of the apartment ajar. "Who was that you were arguing with?"

He passed her in silence and hung up his coat and jacket on the coat-rack.

"Aren't you speaking to me any more? I asked who you were arguing with."

"And I didn't answer!" He himself was startled by his loud tone of voice.

She snapped in a whisper: "You shouldn't shout like that! What will people think?"

"I don't care a fart what they think!"

"Don't be so vulgar. What's the matter with you?" She followed him into the bedroom. "Was it Frau Kannegiesser?"

"Frau Kannegiesser, Frau Kannegiesser!" He sat down on the bed and undid his shoelaces. "Stuff Frau Kannegiesser."

"Don't be so common!" She pulled her cardigan together over her breast. "I've told you hundreds of times that business with the cat won't do. If it gets scared in the basket it'll go frantic, and then it might attack someone. You must carry it down when it has to go out."

Scholten picked up a slipper suddenly and threw it at the wardrobe. There was a heavy hollow thud.

"Joseph!" cried Hilde in a shrill anxious voice. She put her hand over her mouth. "Have you gone out of your mind?"

He jumped up, went into the kitchen, almost falling over his shoelaces, and caught himself up against the fridge. He took a bottle of beer out of it, put it to his lips and drank half of it. He belched noisily and at length.

He didn't see Hilde. She was out in the corridor. "This is too much!" she whispered.

"What did you say?" He raised the bottle again.

She looked round the kitchen door. "You should be ashamed of yourself. You're only acting like this because you know I hate it. You know it makes me feel ill."

140

He clutched the bottle to his chest, drew in his chin, blew out his cheeks. Only at the second attempt did he manage to belch, but then it was good and loud.

Hilde sobbed. "You must be crazy." Her mouth was trembling. "How can you be so horrible? What's happened?"

"Nothing. Nothing at all. Everything's perfectly normal."

She gulped. "I expect Herr Wallmann's been bullying you again, and now you want to take it out on me."

He looked at her. "On you? I don't want to take anything out on you."

"Yes, you do. Your anger. You want to take it out on me because you can't open your mouth in front of Herr Wallmann."

He looked at her.

She returned his glance and said: "You don't dare stand up to Herr Wallmann. You're too cowardly. You've been a coward all your life. That's why you never made good."

He turned away, put his foot up on the chair and tied his shoelace.

Her voice rose, high and shrill. "What are you doing? You're not going out again, are you?"

He tied the other shoelace, passed her in the corridor and put his jacket and coat on.

She stood in the kitchen doorway, both hands clutching at her cardigan. "Joseph, take your shoes off again at once! You're staying here, Joseph!"

He passed her, opened the front door of the apartment. Voice half-choked with fear, she said: "But Joseph, supper's ready!"

As he went downstairs he heard her sobbing wildly behind him.

19

He got into his car and went to the brothel. After half
an hour he came out. He drove into the city centre and
found a place to park in a steep alleyway.

He climbed up the cobblestones of the road surface.
The narrow strip of sky above was still light, a melting
mixture of green and blue. Lighted windows glowed in
the crumbling black façades. Kids were playing in the
entrance to a yard. Foreign kids. He had lived in a
building like that with his parents before they got the
apartment from the cooperative on the other side of
the river.

There'd been a knocking-shop here too. They
mainly passed it by when they came away from bowling. Sometimes they went in, but only for a couple of
beers and short drinks for the girls. You couldn't do
much in such a big crowd. You went along with the
others, and a few times they'd been flung out when the
women realized they weren't wanted.

Scholten took a deep breath. Garlic. Well, it didn't
smell much better here in the past. Pickled beans.
And it always used to stink of piss too. This really
didn't smell so bad. They were probably frying
mutton.

He felt hungry. He climbed up to the old city gate,
went along the narrow high street. Warm fug drifted
out of the bars. He came to the narrow building where
his Uncle Franz once had an ironmonger's shop. It was
a Turkish butcher's now. Unrecognizable. A sheep's

head surrounded by little red lights goggled at him from the display window.

Scholten's fingers felt the sharp iron hooks let into the windowsill. He had never understood what they were for, but probably to keep people from sitting on the windowsill; the shop window might have been broken.

In spite of the hooks he did sometimes sit on the sill, supported on both hands so that the hooks didn't dig in. On summer evenings; that was when he'd had to leave school and Uncle Franz took him on as a trainee. Uncle Franz closed the shop at seven, but there was always clearing up to do, and he liked young Jupp to stay and help out.

Little Jupp certainly stayed when Aunt Gertrud had something special for supper. Fried potato pancakes or pork knuckle with sauerkraut. She would tell him the day before, and Jupp would tell his parents, and then he was allowed to stay to supper with Uncle Franz and Aunt Gertrud and come home afterwards. If it was taking Uncle Franz a long time to clear up, Jupp would ask if he could go out for a walk, and Uncle Franz would say: "Yes, yes, off you go, lad, get a bit of fresh air. Supper will taste better for it!"

Young Jupp would perch carefully on the shop windowsill and look up and down the narrow street. He used to watch the corner where you turned to go down the alley. He knew what men had in mind when they stopped on that corner, looked, turned to examine the street and then suddenly disappeared down the alley. Sometimes one of the women came up to the corner too and walked up and down for a little while, a cigarette between her fingers.

Ah, those were the days. Scholten looked at the sheep's head. Suddenly he smelled the unmistakable odour of the ironmonger's shop again, the sharp and acrid smell of the ironware, the sweetish grease, the musty smell of the dust on the wooden floor and the shelves. Even at midday it was dim at the back of the long narrow shop.

It was there, in the faint light from the window looking out on the yard, that young Jupp went to find curtain runners for the daughter of the florist next door. She came up behind him, stood close and looked at him bright-eyed. With sudden daring, young Jupp had felt under her skirt. She slapped his face and ran off, but she was back ten minutes later to fetch the curtain runners. Luckily Uncle Franz hadn't realized why she ran away. Or perhaps he was only pretending not to. "Off her head, that silly girl!"

Yes. Young Jupp had found it hard to leave the shop. Of course he was very proud of his Commercial Training certificate. The eagle with the swastika on top of it, and all those signatures below. But he didn't want to do his Reich Labour Service, he'd rather have stayed in the shop with Uncle Franz.

It was shit. And no sooner was he through with Labour Service than they called him up into the Engineers. Stationed first in Giessen. Then Breslau. And then off to Russia. He was nineteen years old, good heavens, and off to Russia. Until 1947. Six years exactly. He'd come back on 22 June 1947. And he had in fact been very lucky. Healthy enough on the whole, just some water on the legs.

He never saw Uncle Franz again. Uncle Franz burned to death with Aunt Gertrud in 1942 when the cellar behind the building was buried under rubble in an air raid, and the rafters they'd used to support the ceiling of the shelter went up in flames.

No war ever again.

144

Shit!

Scholten turned away from the shop window. He went into the nearest bar and sat down at the counter, ordered two beers, two frikadellers and two hamburgers.

The bartender asked, "Where's your friend, then?"

Scholten said: "It's for me."

The bartender asked: "All of it served at once?"

Scholten said: "If you don't mind."

Three black-haired foreigners were standing near him at the bar. When the bartender brought Scholten's order – "One, two, and here's the bar snacks" – one of the three pointed to Scholten and laughed. "You very hungry. And very thirsty."

"That's right," said Scholten and dipped the first frikadeller in mustard. He bit some off and said: "And you great chatterbox."

"What that?"

"You talk a lot. Understand?" Scholten drank his first beer and waved to the bartender.

"I no talk a lot." The foreigner looked at Scholten. "Why you so angry?"

"Me?"

"Yes, you."

One of the other two said: "His wife ran off."

Scholten picked up the first hamburger and said: "Chance would be a fine thing."

The three foreigners laughed. They raised their glasses and drank to him. He raised his own glass and drank. He wiped his mouth and asked: "Where are you boys from, then?"

"Turkey."

"And how long have you been here?"

The first dug his thumb into his chest. "Me four

years." He moved the thumb to one side. "Him two. And him seven."

"Fancy that. Are you planning to stay for good?"

"No, not for good."

"Why not?" Scholten stuffed the rest of the hamburger in his mouth. "You're doing all right here, aren't you?"

"Sure. Earn good money. But at home ... you understand?"

"Yes, yes, I understand. Your own country, yes. You mean it's your own country."

"That's right, own country."

The Turk who had said nothing so far waved to the bartender and pointed to Scholten's empty glasses.

Scholten accepted the beer. He raised his glass and said: "What are your names?"

The first Turk said: "I'm Nedim. He's Tevfik. He's Rükneddin."

"Good God. How can people call their kids names like that? I'm Jupp. Cheers, lads."

The second Turk wiped his moustache and said: "Were you born here, Jupp?"

"Yeah. Right here. Round the corner."

The Turk nodded. "Your own country."

Scholten nodded. "Yes. Once it was." He leaned both hands on the counter, raised his head and sang, "Oh, the old days, the old days in Cologne ..."

The three Turks, fascinated, looked at him. The bartender said: "Cool it. We get songbirds like you every evening." He began clearing the bar.

Scholten said: "Hey, cool it yourself." He passed a hand over his eyes. "Bring us another round."

The second Turk said: "You sing good."

"Yes. I did once. When I was young. Understand?"

"Sure. But you not old yet."

146

"You think not?"

"You still sing good."

"Really?"

After they had drunk his round the Turks thanked him and left. Scholten said they should stay and he'd buy another round. The Turks laughed and said thank you very much, they'd be happy to stay, but it was no good, they had to go home. "Wife wait with supper, understand?" They shook hands, the second slapped him on the back and said: "See you, Jupp."

Scholten said: "Yes, sure, see you, Mustafa."

The barman came over. "Now what? Want another two?

"Two what?"

"Beers. Or a couple more hamburgers?"

"No, no. I'll have a beer."

He let the beer stand a long time as he sat there brooding. Those lads were well off. "Wife wait with supper." And then for bed and a spot of leg-over. Some of those Turkish women were very beautiful. Your own country, yes. What were they after? They had a home, they had all a man needs. Where was *his* home?

Scholten muttered: "Gone, all gone." Bombed, burned, scattered to the winds. When their bodies were fetched up from the cellar Uncle Franz and Aunt Gertrud had been only half their proper size. It was the heat. The people from the medical auxiliary service had lined the corpses up on the pavement.

Did he still have any country of his own? All gone, all in ashes.

And the Turks had taken over what was left. At least they had a home. Where was *his* home? He was never left alone in his apartment. Or at the works either. Hilde, oh yes. He'd picked a right one there. A good thirty of their thirty-six years together had been pure purgatory. Purgatory? No, hell. Hell for certain now Erika was dead.

A wave of heat ran through him. Wallmann. Wallmann would sack him at the next opportunity. The moment he made another slip. And there was nothing he could do about it. Nothing at all. The man had murdered Erika, and he couldn't even report it to the police. He'd done his best, but they were too stupid. And he could do no more if he didn't want to lay himself open to suspicion.

So now the bastard was going to throw him out at the age of fifty-eight. Then he couldn't even drive to work in the morning. He'd be delivered up to Hilde day and night.

He broke out in a sweat. He picked up his glass, emptied it, clutched the counter with both hands.

It couldn't be true. It would do for him.

There must be some way. He must at least keep his job. Otherwise he'd be done for, no doubt of it.

He stared at the glass. Suddenly his eyebrows drew together. He rubbed his forehead hard. He looked absently at the bartender, who was putting a fresh glass down in front of him. "Or didn't you want another?"

It was a little while before Scholten answered. "Yes, sure." He rubbed his forehead again.

Just a moment. There *was* a possibility. Yes, there was.

He couldn't do anything to Wallmann. But could Wallmann do anything to him? He had Wallmann just where he wanted him. After all, he knew what the man had done. Wallmann couldn't touch him. He could shut Wallmann's mouth for him, couldn't he? He had only to drop a hint.

And that would make Wallmann pipe down. Oh yes, Herr Wallmann would be in a cold sweat then.

Scholten picked up his glass, drank, wiped his mouth. His lips twisted into a taut smile.

So suppose next time Herr Wallmann turned nasty he just dropped a hint. "Herr Wallmann, I think you ought to keep your voice down. I think you should be careful, know what I mean? You don't? But you've heard how black ice can be made in the freezer, have you?"

No, maybe not so direct. No need to be so direct anyway. He had only to say: "Can you tell me what happened to those five strips of wood? And the insulating tape? And how the grease got on the bolts – the bolts in the steps, know what I mean? Or would you rather tell the police about it?"

And then Herr Wallmann would turn very quiet. He might even say: "How much do you want?"

Scholten gave a start, looked around. No one was watching him. He waved to the bartender. "Let's have one more." He looked round again. He propped his elbows on the counter, shielded his eyes with his hand.

Funny that he hadn't thought of that before, not at all. Well, obviously not, he was too decent. After all, Jupp Scholten was no blackmailer.

But you could think about such things. And what did blackmail mean in this case anyway? Was Wallmann to get off scot-free? A bastard like that? You couldn't call it blackmail, not with his sort. At the most you'd be depriving him of some of his ill-gotten gains. The money he'd stolen by murder. Murder and robbery. Exactly.

Scholten looked round again. Then he waved to the bartender. "I'll have a cigar."

"Light or black?"

"Black." Scholten chose a black cigar, bit the end off, held it to the match the barman handed him. He puffed, watched the blue clouds rising.

Yes, what a moment! "Or would you rather tell the police about it, Herr Wallmann?" Then Wallmann turns very quiet and asks: "How much do you want?"

And suppose he simply replied, let's say, "A hundred thousand"? Wallmann could easily shell out that much. The whole firm was his now, and the house, and the weekend house by the lake. And the boat.

Yes. That'd be quite something! A hundred thousand. It didn't have to be all at once. A ten thousand advance, perhaps. Like a deposit. And the rest in instalments. A thousand a month. Or two thousand a month. Wallmann could easily afford it.

With that kind of money you could go to Holland for the weekend or even longer, you could really paint the town red. Like when his bowling club was still in existence, and they always went on tour to the seaside. Not too far from Amsterdam, of course. Days in the fresh air among the dunes. Then Amsterdam in the evening. Or one of the seaside bars. Cafés, that's what the Dutch call them. And really paint the town red.

Oh Lord! A hundred thousand. A thousand a month, no need for more. That really would be something.

Scholten noticed a man leaning against the counter, watching him. He felt uncomfortable. He paid and left. He crossed the road, head bent, cigar between his teeth, hands in his coat pockets and went down the alley. The kids were still playing in the entrance to the yard.

As he got into his car a new idea struck him like a blow. He sat there motionless, staring absently through the windscreen.

There was nothing he could do with the money. Nothing worth mentioning anyway. He couldn't spend it. As long as Hilde lived she'd keep him on a tight leash. Go to Holland? Not likely. She wouldn't let him go anywhere. And if he did she'd give him no peace day or night. She'd want to know where all that money came from.

A hundred thousand. Oh, shit. It'd do him no good, not while Hilde was alive. And she'd live a long time, he was sure of that: she would probably outlive him. She was tough as old boots. And if she actually did die first, he wouldn't need Wallmann's money. He'd have the fifty thousand from her life insurance anyway. A hundred thousand in the case of accidental death.

Scholten froze. He sat behind the wheel for some time as if paralysed, hardly breathing. Then he looked round. He rubbed his eyes. He quickly wound the window down, let the cigar smoke out, waved his hand to disperse it. He rubbed his eyes again and then his chin. He left his hand on his chin, motionless, and stared through the windscreen.

He shook his head. What sort of ideas are those, Jupp Scholten? How can you possibly entertain them? You're no Wallmann, are you?

No. No, I'm not. That's the trouble. That's why Erika is dead, and Wallmann has got away with murder, and Hilde's alive, and I'm just a poor bastard. That's what it is.

You can't help thinking about it. Why does a wonderful woman like Erika have to die, and someone like Hilde's still alive? For thirty years she's been saying how sick she is, and how bad she feels, and how hard life is to bear, but she goes on living, she goes on living year after year without stopping. Is that justice? She said it herself, she said it would have been better if she'd fallen down those steps and Erika was still alive. Who knows, perhaps she really would feel better off dead, no more of all those aches and pains, no more need to get upset about him?

Scholten slowly leaned back in his seat.

And as for him, he'd be a free man.

Couldn't you even think about such things?

A hundred thousand in the case of accidental death. If Hilde had an accident and died, he would get a hundred thousand marks.

For instance, if she fell down the steps at the house by the lake.

Surely you could think about such things! What was wrong with that? If Hilde fell down the steps she'd be at peace. And so would he. And he could go to Holland, for instance, as often and for as long as he liked.

Scholten sat up straight. And there was something else too.

He'd be free of Wallmann. For the rest of his life.

Just a moment. Think it all over carefully, Jupp Scholten. Nothing wrong with thinking about it, was there? The Lord God never said you mustn't think.

He cleared his throat and stared through the windscreen.

Suppose he took Hilde with him next time he went to the house by the lake. He only had to do exactly what Wallmann had done. No one would ever find out. No one had found out what Wallmann did, not even the police. Only Jupp Scholten.

He just had to make sure Hilde went down the steps. But there must be some way of doing that. He could say he still had something to do on the boat. And if he didn't come back she'd go down the steps to see what he was up to. "What are you doing, Joseph?"

And then all the misery would be over.

No one would work out what had happened.

Except Wallmann.

Wallmann would know why Hilde had fallen down the steps. But he couldn't say. Because if he did he'd be giving himself away. Wallmann would realize that Scholten knew how Erika had her accident. And he could think himself lucky he didn't have to fork out for that too.

Wallmann would leave him in peace for the rest of his life.

Scholten passed his hand over his face. He took a deep breath. Then he started the engine and drove off.

As he was about to turn into his own street he stamped on the brake hard. Then he put his foot on the accelerator and went on again. "Oh, hell!" he swore. "Oh, bloody hell."

He drove twice round the block then went a couple of streets further and finally stopped outside a bar. He stayed sitting in the dark, rubbing his chin.

He had overlooked an important point. It couldn't work. If he were to do it, and he had no intention of doing it, but *if* he were to do it, there'd be a problem that had not faced Wallmann. Or rather, it had faced Wallmann. But Wallmann had been able to solve it.

The alibi.

Jupp Scholten would have no excuse for driving back into town. No files, no bowling club. No Sauerborn to take him home.

Hilde wouldn't be going into Grandmontagne's either. She wouldn't be buying meat or drinking grog. She'd be going away with him, her Joseph, sticking to him like a burr, she wouldn't leave his side for a moment if possible. He'd have to take her to the house with him. No one would be able to swear she'd been sitting in the village bar alive and well drinking grog while he was already on his way back to town.

He could do everything else just like Wallmann, but the waterproof alibi wasn't available. Not to Jupp Scholten.

Bloody hell.

He groaned out loud, and was startled by the sound emerging from his chest. He stared at the windows of the bar.

Well, it had only been a crazy idea anyway. He hadn't really wanted to do it. He wouldn't have done it. It had been just a flight of fancy.

He pulled himself together, got out of the car. He stood there, holding the door handle. Then he slapped his forehead and laughed.

It had all been nonsense anyway. How could he have thought up all that stuff?

Wallmann would never send him up to the house again in any case. Not after that business with the reporter. That was all over now.

He locked the car and went into the bar.

20

There was a spell of fine weather in mid-October. Blue skies, bright sunshine by day, although it turned very cold at night. The air was clear at the office. No complications. Wallmann was behaving tolerably well.

One Monday afternoon he summoned Scholten into his office. He offered him the cigar box. "Like one?"

"If I may," said Scholten, choosing a cigar.

Wallmann said: "I'm going away for a few days tomorrow."

"Oh yes?" Scholten turned the cigar in his fingers, passed it back and forth under his nose. Wallmann's bit of fluff had gone on holiday on Friday. For two and a half weeks.

Wallmann cleared his throat. "Yes, for a couple of weeks. I need a few days' relaxation."

"Are you taking the boat?"

"No, no. It gets boring on the lake for that long. And it's too cold now. No, I'm flying to the Bahamas."

"Good heavens."

Wallmann shifted position in the chair at his desk. "At least I can sail properly there."

"Sure."

Wallmann cleared his throat again. "What I wanted to ask is, could you go up again while I'm away and see to the boat? It's time to put it to bed for the winter. I won't be able to do the job myself. All this came up quite suddenly – going away, I mean. If you'd get the boat ready then I can take it into the yachting basin as soon as I get back."

Scholten realized that he was crushing the cigar. He placed it carefully on Wallmann's desk, put both hands in his overall pockets. "Well, I'll have to talk to my wife. What exactly would you like me to do?"

"I looked out last year's checklist." Wallmann took a piece of paper off his desk and handed it to Scholten.

Scholten looked at the list. "I don't know that I can do all that in one day. And if I'm up there anyway, I might as well get the weeds out."

"I don't mind if it takes you two days. I'll pay you."

"Yes, but we have a lot to do here at the moment. All the balance sheets."

"I know, so why not go at the weekend and take your wife? If you leave here a little early on Friday you'll be through with the work by Saturday evening, and then you can relax on Sunday. I think the weather will hold, and it's beautiful up there at this time of year. It will do your wife good."

"Yes, I'll make sure I can manage it."

Wallmann took two hundred-mark notes from his wallet then added another two. "That's for the materials. You can tell me what they came to when I'm back."

"Yes, right." Scholten took the money. "Thanks very much," he said.

Hilde concealed her pleasure by asking how much longer he was going to let Herr Wallmann impose on him. She said she didn't know if she could take the strain of it all, she'd been feeling very unwell all day.

When Scholten came home on Tuesday evening she had already packed. She said the packing had left her very stressed; it was just amazing what Herr Wallmann expected of him.

156

Scholten said he'd go to the DIY store after work on Thursday and buy the materials; drive them straight over to the house and get everything ready so that it wouldn't take him so long on Friday and Saturday. Then they could fit in a walk on Saturday as well.

Hilde was against this idea. She said he could buy the materials during office hours on Friday; it was Herr Wallmann's boat, after all. And then she said he only wanted to go over on Thursday so that he'd have at least one evening alone up there, and he wouldn't be getting anything ready because he'd be sitting around in Grandmontagne's bar half the night.

Scholten said Grandmontagne didn't open on Thursdays, he'd told her so hundreds of times. And he hadn't said he was planning to spend the night at the house either; he could be back around nine or ten in the evening. But if she didn't like it, and as usual he was sure she knew best, then he'd give up the idea of the whole trip, he'd only agreed for her sake anyway, he could well do without it, and Herr Wallmann would have to see about putting his boat to bed for the winter himself.

On Thursday at midday Scholten called the Meteorological Office in Essen. During the lunch break, when Rosa had disappeared into Büttgenbach's little room, he went into Inge Faust's office, dialled Directory Enquiries with trembling fingers and asked for the number. He wrote it on a scrap of paper, put it in his overall pocket, looked out into the corridor again and listened for anyone who might be coming before he called the Met Office. A man with an impressive bass voice told him that unless something unforeseen happened, the weather would hold over the weekend. Scholten asked: "Could there be frost?"

The man said: "It's possible. Near water, you understand."

Scholten was bathed in sweat by the time he was back at his desk. He tore the note into tiny scraps and threw them in the wastepaper basket. He looked out of the window. He began to count on his fingers, silently moving his lips. After a while he nodded. He nodded several times. When he heard Rosa coming he picked up his papers and began hastily looking through them.

At three he went to see Büttgenbach and said Herr Wallmann had told him to deal with the boat. He was just off to buy the materials and take them straight up to the house, there were a few things he had to get ready there, or he wouldn't get it all done at the weekend.

Büttgenbach said: "Herr Wallmann never said anything about today. He just said you might be leaving a little early on Friday."

Scholten asked when, in that case, he was supposed to buy the materials? Had Herr Büttgenbach any idea of the crowds at the DIY store on a Friday afternoon? And he didn't want to spend the whole weekend working on the boat. He supposed he had a right to a little time off. However, if Herr Büttgenbach had anything against it he'd stay here, and if he wasn't finished with the boat by Sunday evening that was just Herr Wallmann's bad luck.

Büttgenbach said: "I never said I had anything against it." He opened a file and immersed himself in reading it.

Scholten drove to the DIY store and looked out the materials for Wallmann's boat. Then he bought a roll of insulating tape, twelve yards. Before he started along the motorway he stopped off at a supermarket. He put three bottles of beer in his shopping trolley, thought about it and added a fourth. In the meat section he chose a fillet steak. Then he looked at the salads and decided on a medium head of lettuce.

Just before six he drove up to the garage. It was almost dark already. The vault of the sky was blue, turning to a pale green towards the west. The first stars were twinkling on the eastern side of the great dome of the heavens, above the black crest of the woods. A cold breeze blew in off the lake.

Scholten carried his provisions into the house and put the beer in the fridge, taking one bottle with him; it was cold enough. He left the materials for the boat in the garage.

Then he chose five of the remaining wooden strips. Using the circular saw, he cut ten lengths of twenty-eight inches and ten of twelve inches each. He put the remnants on the hearth and lit the fire.

When he came out the sky was dark blue in the west as well. Scholten went around the house once, stopped, listened. Nothing to be heard. The starlight cast a faint glow on the roof of the house, on the tree-tops, filling the air.

Scholten shivered. He took out his handkerchief, mopped his brow and the back of his neck with it. He put the handkerchief away. He stood there for a moment longer, listening again. Then he quickly went into the garage.

He took the bolts out of their tin and put them in his pocket. He found a long-armed spanner, tested it to see if it fitted tightly enough on the nuts for the bolts. Then he took three of the old planks out to the steps.

About fifty minutes later he had changed over the three planks of the landing and the two steps above it, had taken the planks he had removed into the garage, put insulating tape on the edges of the planks, nailed the strips over it. His back and belly were dripping with sweat. His back was trembling too as he bent to check the slope of the little basins he had made.

He cleared the contents of the freezer into the two coolbags, filled his basins with water and put them carefully in the freezer, one by one. He propped the lowest on two pieces of wood and stacked the other four on top, pointing in different directions, so that there would be room for the shanks of the bolts below the planks.

He closed the freezer and looked around the garage. All in order. His lettuce was washed and dressed at a quarter to eight, when Scholten put the fillet steak in the pan.

When he had eaten and drunk he sat down in the living room with the last bottle of beer. He planned to switch the TV on. He sat there for a while.

Suddenly he felt his heart beating, beating hard in his throat. He cleared his throat to break the silence. His own ears heard the hard fast beating of his heart.

21

He finished his beer, locked up the house, glanced round the garage again and drove away. At eight-thirty he rang the doorbell of Grandmontagne's house. Marlene opened the door. "Hey, what are you doing here?" she asked. Grandmontagne came out of the living room in his slippers.

Scholten said he'd be back tomorrow evening, he had to get the boat ready for winter over the weekend. He was bringing his wife with him.

"Good God!" said Grandmontagne. "Well, have a nice weekend. See you some other time."

Scholten laughed. He asked if Grandmontagne could get him some meat for goulash, a pound of best braising steak would be about right, and three-quarters of a pound of ground beef for steak tartare, four pork and beef sausages, and half a pound of sliced cooked meats. And a piece of fine liver sausage, not too small.

"Sure, Jupp," said Grandmontagne, "you can collect it when you drive up tomorrow evening. Write it down, Marlene."

Scholten asked if the boy couldn't bring it over to the house when the shop closed. His wife, he said, always had problems after a drive, she didn't take car journeys well, she always had to go and lie down when she arrived, and if he stopped off at Grandmontagne's there was bound to be a great fuss.

Grandmontagne said: "Oh, you don't need to say no

more, that's okay, Jupp, the lad will bring it up around quarter to seven."

Marlene said: "Why don't you drive slower, then? Show a bit of consideration for your wife!"

Scholten was home soon after ten. Hilde was in bed, with the bedroom door open and the bedside lamp switched on. She said she didn't know if she'd be able to stand up to the drive. She'd been feeling very ill all day.

On Friday afternoon Scholten left the office at a quarter to three. Herr Büttgenbach looked at him askance but said nothing. Kurowski called: "Mind how you go, Herr Scholten, know what I mean? Don't do anything I wouldn't do!"

"You must be joking," said Scholten. "I'm taking my wife with me."

"Have fun, then," said Rothgerber.

Rosa shook her head. "Do mind out, Herr Scholten."

"Mind out for what?"

"Mind you don't fall in the water."

"Not me."

When he got home Hilde was waiting in the corridor with her hat and coat already on. He carried the suitcase and travelling bag downstairs. Then he came up again, put the cat in the cat basket and took it to the car. He put the basket on the back seat, between the travelling bag and the back of Hilde's seat. Hilde said: "That's too much of a crush. Can't you put the basket behind your seat?" He put the basket behind his seat.

He drove very fast. Hilde said he ought to drive more slowly; it was making her feel all hot. He went not very much more slowly. Once off the motorway he drove jerkily, letting the car skid on bends. He said it was because of the road. "The whole surface needs renewing, it's dangerous. But they just come with a bucket of tar in spring and paint it over the holes. Another botched job."

They reached the house at a quarter past five. He unlocked, and Hilde lay down on the living-room sofa at once. He emptied the car and unpacked the case and the bag.

He was going to light the fire on the hearth, but Hilde said: "Don't. We're not having that fire lit."

He stood there, matchbox in hand. "Why not?"

"It makes such a stink. My eyes won't stand the smoke. You know they won't."

"The fire doesn't smoke. It'll warm the place up and do you good."

"The central heating's warm enough. It's far too hot in here anyway." She threw off the rug she had spread over her feet. "If it's too cold for you, you can put your cardigan on."

He stood there undecided for a moment, then put the matches away. "Well, I'll go to the garage now and down to the boat after that," he said. "The boy's bringing up the meat from Grandmontagne's at quarter to seven. I ordered beef for steak tartare for this evening."

"Are you going to stay on the boat that long? It's getting dark, you won't be able to see a thing."

"There's electric light on the boat."

"That's right, let Herr Wallmann impose on you! Not that that's anything new. You're nothing but Herr Wallmann's odd-job man."

He stopped, stood in the doorway, looked at her. Then he turned and went out.

He looked in the freezer. The ice on the planks was hard and smooth as glass. He took the long-armed spanner off the workbench and went down to the steps. Leaving the spanner on the landing, he went on down to the boat. He opened up the cabin and switched on the interior light.

The battery would be run down when he came back, but there was nothing to be done about that. Herr Wallmann wouldn't say a thing. He'd keep his mouth shut all right.

Scholten had the icy steps in place just before six-thirty. The strips of wood he had knocked away from the planks were underneath the other spare strips. He had hidden the lengths of insulating tape in a cardboard carton among other small items. He had put the substitute planks back in their corner in the garage, had taken the frozen food out of the coolbags and put it back in the freezer.

Every time he made another journey to or from the steps, hurrying, stumbling, gasping under the weight he carried, he had stolen up to the corner of the living-room window and looked in, his heart beating fast. Hilde was lying on the sofa with her eyes closed. She had wrapped the rug firmly round her legs and pulled it up to her chin.

Scholten looked round the garage. All in order. He brushed the dust off his pullover and trousers, looked at his hands. They were so cold they hurt. He had scratched the skin in a couple of places. He licked the scratches. He looked at his watch. High time.

He went into the living room. Hilde opened her eyes. "I'm going to put the car away in the garage now and then go down to the boat," he said.

"You told me so already. Haven't you finished yet?"

"Another half an hour. I'll be back when you have the steak tartare ready."

He put the cat in the cat basket. It stuck its paw out of the top before he closed the lid.

"What are you putting the cat in the basket for?"

"Taking it down to the boat. It'll be a bit of company."

"Are you mad? You can't take the cat on the boat with you! It won't like the rocking. It'll be sick."

"Oh, come off it!" He stood in the doorway with the basket in his hand. He looked at her.

She said: "Oh, yes, of course you know best as usual. The fact is you don't know anything." She closed her eyes. "A know-all, that's you, nothing but a know-all."

He turned away and closed the door.

Carefully, he opened the fridge and took out a carton of milk. He took one of the old cups out of the kitchen cupboard. Without a sound, he removed his jacket and coat from the coat-rack and put them over his arm. He closed the front door and looked through the living-room window once more. Hilde was lying on the sofa with her eyes closed.

His hands began to shake. He stood there for ten or twenty seconds. Suddenly he looked at his watch. Damn it, time to get moving. He threw his coat and jacket into the car, stowed the cat basket in front of the passenger seat. He put the carton of milk and the cup in the glove compartment. He looked round once again. A strip of reddish light fell from the living-room window on the ground in front of the garage.

He started the engine and drove not into the garage but down the track leading to the road. A little way from the house he stopped, ran back, pushed the garage door down and made sure that it engaged in the lock with a loud slam. He stole back to the living-room window once more. Hilde was still lying there motionless. He passed both hands over his face then went back to his car.

He took off the handbrake and let the car coast

down the path. The bodywork shook and creaked. Only just before reaching the road did he start the engine. He drove towards the village, turned into the dark square by the little transformer station, switched off the engine and the lights. He wound down the window and breathed deeply to calm his thudding heart.

He didn't have to wait long. Headlights were approaching from the village. Scholten saw Grandmontagne's delivery van drive past. He started the car again at once and drove into the village, parking outside Grandmontagne's long, low house. He took the basket out of the car and went into the pub.

Two men were sitting at the corner table. Grandmontagne was behind the bar. He wiped his hands down and said: "Hey, what's up? I thought you was here with your wife. The boy's just gone over with your meat."

"I know." Scholten put the basket down on the bar. "He passed me on the way. Let's have a beer, Sheng."

Grandmontagne drew the beer. He looked up from the glass, glanced at Scholten. "This means trouble, mate."

Scholten made a dismissive gesture. "Who cares? I can't be in more trouble than I'm in already. I can tell you, Sheng, it's sheer hell with that woman. The fuss she's just been kicking up again – you wouldn't believe it. She makes my life hell, she really does. I've had it, Sheng, I've had it up to here!"

Grandmontagne nodded.

Scholten said: "I'd like to drop it all and just walk out. Get in the car and go anywhere. Somewhere peaceful. To Holland. Somewhere by the sea, where I wouldn't see or hear any more of her."

Grandmontagne put the beer down in front of

166

Scholten. He said: "Well, you just do that. Why not, eh? Your old lady will be okay. Got everything up there she could need. Even the meat and the sausage now. You take off – that won't half shake her up!"

Scholten emptied his glass. He put it down violently on the bar. "You carry on like that much longer and I swear I really *will* do it."

Grandmontagne took the glass and refilled it. He looked at the head on the beer. "Like I said, you just do that," he said. "You got to show a woman you're your own master, Jupp. Or you've had it. For good."

One of the two men in the corner said: "Let's have the telly on, Sheng. Take a look at the news."

"What for? It ain't as if you understood it." But Grandmontagne went over to the corner and switched the TV set on. He came back, gave Scholten his beer and pointed to the basket. "What you got in there? Packed a picnic for the journey already?"

"I should have done. No, it's my cat in there." Scholten opened the lid, and the cat looked out. It rose and looked as if it was about to jump up on the bar. "No, Manny." Scholten tickled the cat's neck, and it began to purr.

"Why drag that animal round with you?"

Scholten stroked the cat. He held a finger in front of its nose. The cat raised a paw, put its head on one side and snapped at the finger. Scholten said: "She hit it with a shoe, that's why."

"What, your wife did?"

Scholten nodded.

"I don't believe it!" Grandmontagne shook his head. "Didn't know she were violent too. Poor dumb animal. Can't help nothing, can it?"

Scholten said: "Do you have a drop of milk?"

Grandmontagne went to the kitchen door and

called: "Marlene, let's have a saucer of milk here. No, a cupful."

Marlene's voice came from the kitchen. "What for?"

"Jupp's got his cat with him."

Marlene Grandmontagne appeared in the kitchen doorway, hands on her hips. "What's all this, then? I thought you was here with your wife."

"Never mind gabbing." Grandmontagne flapped his hand. "Fetch that milk."

When Marlene brought the milk Scholten put the cat down on the floor. Marlene, hands on her hips again, looked at the cat, looked at Scholten. "What're you taking the cat around for, then?"

The boy came in through the door out to the street, empty butcher's basket over his arm. "Oh, Herr Scholten!" he said. "Your wife thought you was on the boat. She were going to call you in for supper."

A wave of heat passed through Scholten. He opened his mouth, gasped for air.

Grandmontagne said: "You mind your own business." He waved the boy away. "Off you go."

Marlene looked from Grandmontagne to Scholten. "What's going on around here? Taken off without a word to the wife, eh?"

Grandmontagne said: "It's nowt to do with you neither. You let Jupp be. He's having a hard enough time anyway."

"Ho, yes, I'm sure you'll back him up!" The indignant Marlene left them.

"Cheers, Jupp." Grandmontagne gave Scholten another beer, raised his own glass. He drank, wiped his mouth, leaned over the bar. "Hey, can't you take me to Holland too? That'd be good, eh?" He laughed, looked at Scholten. "Where'll we go, then?"

Scholten nodded absently.

168

Grandmontagne slapped him on the arm, shook him. "Hey, what's up? Pull yourself together! Take that cat and go! Just get out! See what she says then!"

Scholten nodded. He said: "Do you know Heemswijk?"

"No, where is it?"

"By the seaside. There are woods. Woods all over the dunes. You can walk there for hours. On the beach if you'd rather, or in the woods if you like."

"They got good beer there too?" Grandmontagne leaned forward. "And nice little girlies?"

Scholten waved a hand. "Any number. Amsterdam's not far off."

"Amsterdam? Hey, that'd be the place for me. What are we waiting for, Jupp?"

Scholten nodded. "We always used to go there with the bowling club. Every year. I can tell you, we had a good time." He nodded. "Yes, and then the women went on and on at us, and in the end the club closed."

Grandmontagne took his shoulder, shook him. "Don't let 'em get you down, Jupp, you hear me?"

Scholten nodded. "Yes, sure." He looked around. The cat was rubbing round the two men in the corner. "Manny, come here! Leave them alone. Good boy, come on." He bent down, snapped his fingers. The cat came over and rubbed its head on his hand. Scholten asked: "What's the time, Sheng?"

"Twenty past seven exactly. Like another?"

"No, thanks." Scholten picked up the cat and put it in the basket.

"Feeling nervous?"

Scholten nodded. He took out his handkerchief and wiped his brow, his mouth and the back of his neck.

"I guess you do," said Grandmontagne.

169

Scholten took out his wallet, but Grandmontagne waved it aside. "Forget it, Jupp. On the house."

Scholten nodded. "My turn next time."

"Yeah, that's okay. Look out for yourself."

Scholten picked the cup up from the floor, put it on the bar. He closed the basket and started off.

As he opened the door he turned back and nodded.

"Give my regards to Holland!" said Grandmontagne. He laughed, dried his hands. When the door had closed behind Scholten he leaned on the bar, shaking his head.

Scholten put the basket back in front of the passenger seat. He stared through the windscreen. Suddenly a sob shook him. He swallowed, rubbed both hands hard over his face. He stared through the windscreen again.

It was too late. He had no option now.

He started the engine. He did not turn but drove straight out of the village, going very fast. He braked only briefly before the bends, changing down and then driving on with the engine roaring.

If the filling station in the little town had closed he was in trouble.

But the filling station was open. He got the tank filled right up, stood beside the car. "Bloody cold this evening, eh?"

The attendant shrugged his shoulders. "Winter's on its way."

"How long are you on duty here?"

"Until ten. No one comes by after then."

Scholten nodded. "They wouldn't. Could you look at the oil too? I want to get to Holland this evening."

He stood there until the filling-station attendant had finished then followed him into the warm shop, paid, got a receipt.

"Do you have the exact time?" he asked.

The attendant compared the clock on the wall with his watch. "Exactly twenty to eight," he said. Scholten looked at his own watch, nodded. He said: "Can I phone from here?" He felt hot. Sweat suddenly broke out in his armpits.

The attendant pointed to the corner. Scholten lifted the receiver, dialled the number of the weekend house. The first time he misdialled. His finger got stuck and he shifted the phone. He tried again, slowly. This time he succeeded.

He stood there with the receiver to his ear, listening to the ringing tone. He heard his heart beating fast and hard. He felt as if distant music were reaching his ear down the phone, mysterious and polyphonic. He held his breath. He was afraid of staggering, and supported himself with one hand on the wall.

Fear clutched at his heart.

He opened his mouth, took a deep breath. The idea that he might have misdialled again went through his mind. He pressed the receiver rest down, was about to dial again, stopped. Fingers trembling, he unbuttoned his coat, took his notebook out of his jacket pocket. His chequebook came with it and fell to the floor. He picked up the chequebook, put the notebook on the table and looked up the number of the weekend house.

He dialled very carefully, digit by digit.

The ringing tone, for a very long time. And after a while that damn music drifted into his ear again. He shuddered. He let the receiver fall back on the rest.

The attendant was sitting behind his little desk, tilting his chair back and forth and chewing a match. "Nobody home?"

"No. No, there's no answer." Scholten put the notebook away, buttoned up his coat. "Thanks very much. Have a nice weekend."

"Thanks, and the same to you."

He sat in his car for one or two minutes as if paralysed. Suddenly he started the engine and drove away at high speed. When he was on the motorway he put his foot down. The road was empty, endless, cold under the sparkling starry sky.

After a while Scholten had to drive more slowly. Tears were blurring his eyes. He wiped them away, steering with one hand, but more and more kept coming. He drove onto the hard shoulder, stopped, looked for his handkerchief. He said, his voice stifled: "Don't do anything silly, Jupp Scholten, you've got to get out of here. Come on!" He blew his nose hard, wiped his eyes. He put his foot down and drove on.

At eight-fifteen he reached the border crossing. As he slowly approached the brightly lit glass cabins he leaned to one side, lifted the lid of the cat basket and put one finger in. He felt the cat's nose. It began nibbling at his finger with its sharp teeth. "Be a good boy now, Manny," he said. "Not a peep out of you, understand?"

He was prepared for them to look inside the basket and ask to see a veterinary certificate. Then he'd have to drive back and look for a hotel at the next exit.

The customs man looked at the photo in Scholten's passport, gave it back and said: "Have a good trip."

Scholten said: "You're friendly for a customs man!"

"Why? Had bad experiences, have you?"

Scholten laughed. "Sometimes, yes."

The man said: "You would with me too if you have anything in the car that shouldn't be there."

Scholten was alarmed. He laughed. "No, no, for God's sake. Nothing to declare!"

"That's okay, then."

Scholten stepped on the accelerator, then braked, put his head out of the window again. "Do you have the right time?"

The man raised his hand. "Look, the big clock there. Eight twenty-one."

Scholten drove to the end of the long parking place. He put the cat on its leash, walked it up and down in the twilight. It inspected the grass for a while, then stopped, raised its tail, twitched the tip of the tail and stared at the darkness. He said: "Get on with it, Manny, we don't have all night."

When the cat had done its business he put it back in the basket. He thought for a moment then closed the lid. Too much milk might not be a good thing now. He drove back and went to the Bureau de Change. He made out a cheque for three hundred marks and had it changed into Dutch gulden. He asked the girl sitting sleepily behind her counter: "Do you have a phone here?"

She raised her chin. "Behind you."

He went into one of the three open phone boxes, put money in the slot, dialled the number of the week-end house. He stared at the dial.

The ringing tone, monotonous, again and again. He felt fear spread through him, suppressing every other thought and movement.

After he had listened to the ringing tone for almost a minute, he hung up. He rubbed his eyes, leaned against the phone. Then he went out. He was staggering and had to reach for the door handle twice.

22

Scholten reached the outer suburbs of Amsterdam around ten. He drove into the city centre. He got lost twice, but finally he recognized the Oude Kerk in the subdued street lighting. He drove up the side of the canal, over a steep narrow bridge and down the canal again along the opposite quay. A car was moving out just in front of him. Scholten went into the parking place it left free.

He took the basket out of the car and slowly climbed the bridge leading over to the Oude Kerk. Reflections of light wandered over the dark, restless water. He stopped, put the basket carefully on the balustrade of the bridge and held it steady with both hands.

It was just like the old days. The tall, narrow, slightly crooked houses on both sides of the canal. Not many of the upper windows were lit, but there was a reddish glow from the basements. The door of the bar on the corner opened, and a clamour of voices came out. Scholten took a deep breath. The air was cold, not as full of aromas as on a summer evening, but there was a faint smell of frying in it, of beer and cigarettes and the musty odour of silt on the walls of the quay, the vapours rising from the dark water.

He felt a sense of promise, just as he had before. Something exciting was going to happen tonight. It was waiting ahead of him somewhere, just round the corner. He felt the excitement in his belly and his legs.

He was breathing hard. He raised the lid of the

basket slightly. "Take a look, Manny. This is Amsterdam. Do you like it?" The cat put its nose out through the crack.

The tower of the Oude Kerk struck the half-hour, ten-thirty, two hoarse, broken notes that echoed back in the ravine of the canal and from the walls of the old church. He put the cat gently back and closed the basket. "No time now, Manny, you can have another look later."

He hurried on with the basket. He found a small hotel in a side street. The paint was peeling off the façade, the steps up to the door were worn. A Moluccan with spiky hair was sitting at the desk in front of the board of keys, reading the newspaper. He wanted twenty-five gulden in advance. Scholten paid and took the key of his room. He said: "I'll be going out again. For a walk, understand?"

The Moluccan smiled and nodded.

"How long is the door open? *De deur open, du verstaan?*"

"*De heele nacht.*" The Moluccan smiled. All night.

"Fine." Scholten was already in the doorway with his basket. He turned. "What's the time? The exact time, *du verstaan?*" He tapped his watch with his finger. The Moluccan looked at his own watch and then at Scholten's. He tapped Scholten's watch. "*Die gaat goed. Achttien minuten voor elf.*" It keeps good time. Eighteen minutes to eleven.

"*Ah, ja, achttien.* Eighteen to eleven. Fine."

He went along the canal in search of a bar. The one on the corner was too full for him; he was afraid it would be too noisy for the cat. He walked over the cobblestones, looking keenly all around him, drawing in the air.

He stopped by the steps leading down to a base-ment. A woman was sitting behind the window at the bottom of the steps. From above, he could see her big breasts in her basque. She looked up, waved to him. He was about to go on, stopped, undecided.

He might not feel so fit afterwards.

He walked a little way further, then turned and went down the steps. The woman opened the door and smiled at him.

He asked: "How much? You *verstaan*?" He rubbed thumb and forefinger together.

She said: "*Vijftig gulden.*"

"*Vijftig?*" He raised the five fingers of one hand. "Fifty?"

She nodded. He went in. As he was taking off his jacket, she tapped the basket. "*Wat heb je er in? Eieren?*" What do you have in there? Eggs?

"In the basket? No, not eggs. You must think I come from the country. No, it's my cat in there."

"Cat? *'n kat? Dat is niet waar!*" A cat? I don't believe it! She opened the lid. The cat rose, arched its back and mewed. The woman began to laugh heartily, picked the cat up, stroked it, went to the door and called, "*Sonja! Kom, kijk eens! 'n kat! Die kerel heft zijn kat bij zich!*" Come and look at this! A cat! The man's brought his cat with him!

In the end there were four women standing around the cat, passing it from one to the other, stroking it and meanwhile looking at Scholten and laughing. Scholten, who was sitting on the bed and had already taken one shoe off, didn't quite know what to do. As if casually he put the shoe on again.

One of the women went to fetch milk for the cat. They bent down and cooed at the animal as it lapped the milk. Scholten watched the broad behind, clad only in knickers, stretched very close to his eyes. He felt rather uncomfortable.

176

It was a good quarter of an hour before the other women left the room. Scholten would really have preferred one of them, a tall blonde, to his hostess, but he doubted whether he could go back on the deal now, and he lacked the vocabulary to explain. The women took the cat with them. Scholten wanted to stop them, but he didn't know how to get his way without raising his voice. The women laughed, waved to him and disappeared with the cat.

For Scholten, it was a fiasco. After ten minutes his hostess shook her head. "*Dat gaat niet. Kijk eens.*" It's not going to work. She raised her hand then lowered it. "*Heb je gedronken?*" Have you been drinking?

Scholten got up. He reached for his trousers and asked, "Where's my cat?"

She went to the door and called: "Sonja?" She went out.

Scholten quickly got dressed and followed her, feeling anxious. The women were kneeling down round the cat in the room on the other side of the narrow corridor. The cat was sitting on the floor, eating chopped raw meat.

Scholten waited until it had finished the last piece and was licking its whiskers. He put the cat in the basket and closed the lid. He said "Thanks. Good evening," and left. The women laughed and called: "*Tot ziens!*" See you soon.

Out in the street he swore softly. Fifty gulden for the cat. He laughed. Yes, for the cat's dinner. He walked past the Oude Kerk, looking up at the mighty stones of the plinth. It was dark down here. He glanced up at the sky.

He whispered: "Just as well."

Perhaps Hilde was dead already. He shivered. He hoped she was dead. He hoped she wasn't suffering any more. He shook his head, whispered: "Jupp Scholten, what a bastard you are!" On the night of Hilde's death.

No, it was just as well he hadn't been able to do it. "You'd never have been able to forgive yourself, Jupp Scholten."

He went on, walking faster. He went into a bar. It was rather full, but he found a free place by the counter. He ordered a beer and a chaser of genever, Dutch gin, asked for the menu. He ordered an *Uitsmijter*, ham and fried eggs, because he wasn't sure what the names of the other dishes meant. By the time it came he was on his third beer and his third genever. He shovelled in the ham and fried eggs, ordered his next beer.

After quarter of an hour the others in the bar had found out what was in the basket. The landlady wanted to give the cat some milk and chopped meat, she indicated to Scholten that it couldn't hurt the cat: it was steak. "Beefsteak, good, good, understand?"

Scholten waved the offer away, inflated his cheeks, pushed out his stomach, patted it, pointed to the cat, and said: "The cat's full, *verstaan?* Cat will burst. Ping! *Verstaan?*"

The people laughed. They stroked the cat and bought Scholten a beer and a genever.

After another half hour he sang "Tulips From Amsterdam". The people clapped and cried "Bravo!" One of them asked if he could sing "Why Is the Rhine So Beautiful?" too. Scholten sang "Why Is The Rhine So Beautiful?", and in response to another request "If all the water in the Rhine, if only it was golden wine". The Dutch hummed and sang along with him.

Then Scholten said he would sing a song from his native land. "From home, *Heimat*, you *verstaan?*" The Dutch nodded. "*Ja, ja, over thuis!*"

Scholten sang a folk song from Cologne. When he let the last note die away, the Dutch clapped like mad. A woman at Scholten's side shook her head; her eyes were wet. Scholten took out his handkerchief, wiped his own eyes first then offered it to the woman. She took it, wiped her eyes, gave Scholten a hearty hug and kissed him on both cheeks.

By two in the morning Scholten was hoarse and very drunk. He cried, "Dear friends! Dear friends, my cat and I must go home. We have a long day ahead tomorrow, we go sleep now, *verstaan?*" He put both hands together and laid his head sideways on them. With his head on one side, he overbalanced. The woman and one of the Dutchmen caught him.

The Dutchman asked where he was staying, said he would take him back. Scholten cried: "No, no. We're staying just round the corner, we can do it, easy." At the second attempt he managed to get the cat in the basket. He almost fell out of the door with the basket, caught himself and steered a course to his hotel over the uneven cobblestones. The Dutch who had come outside watched him go. He twice came dangerously close to the canal, but he found his way and reached the hotel without falling over.

He was in bed at two-fifteen. The cat jumped up on the end of the bed, padded around over his feet for a little while and then curled up. Scholten snored noisily.

23

On Saturday morning Scholten woke at eight. He scratched his head at length, eyes closed, then picked up his trousers, took his wallet out of his pocket and counted his money. He got out of bed, put his head under the tap, rubbed it dry, combed his hair with his hands. He put the cat in the basket and left the hotel.

He looked for his car, located it and put a few coins in the parking meter. He took the carton of milk and the cup out of the glove compartment, put the cup down on the road surface and gave the cat milk. Then he went into a café and had breakfast. He ordered an extra portion of sausage and fed it to the cat.

Before leaving the café he put the cat on its leash and then took it for a walk for half an hour.

It was a fresh sparkling morning. The streets were not very crowded yet. Now and then a tram rattled past. Scholten stopped on the bridge over a canal. He heard one of the round-trip tourist boats hooting beyond the canal that flowed into it. He watched as the broad flat boat turned into the main canal, and he waved to the tourists. When the boat had passed under the bridge where he was standing he sighed contentedly.

He put the cat in its basket and looked for a barber's. He had himself shaved and got a haircut. In the warm sweetish air of the shop he fell into a drowsy half-sleep.

He got up feeling pleasantly relaxed.

He went out of the shop, enjoyed the view of the old,

carefully painted and plastered houses. Their window-panes shone. He felt the cool air on his shaved cheeks. His scalp was warm, he could still feel the effects of the massage right down to the nape of his neck.

Scholten went into a tobacconist's and bought a black cigar, lit it from the gas flame. He walked a little way down the road, looked in shop windows, stopped here and there, puffing out little blue clouds of smoke.

He looked at the time. Not even ten yet. He didn't have to leave before two or three in the afternoon. Wallmann had been back at the house just before six that Saturday evening in March. It wouldn't take him more than three and a half hours to drive back.

Suddenly he felt something coming towards him, something unpleasant, irksome, oppressive. Something sinister. Something terrible. He tried to push it out of his mind. He straightened his shoulders, involuntarily swung his arms. But it kept coming closer. He looked in the shop windows, trying to make out his reflection. Other reflections overlaid it. He saw the outline of his figure, his head, the cigar in the corner of his mouth, the basket in his hand. He couldn't see what was behind him.

He turned and went hastily on. He looked at his watch again, stopped. He had plenty of time. He could go out to the sea. He could go for a walk, on the beach, in the woods on the dunes. He would eat lunch at the beach restaurant and leave at two or three. He could easily be back at the weekend house by six.

He hurried back to his car. When he had reached the canal and saw the car on the other side, he realized that however much of a hurry he was in, however fast he drove, the thing that was behind him would still catch up. He stopped, rubbed his face. "Bloody hell." He looked for a phone box.

He put the basket down under the phone. "Yes, Manny, we'll be off in a moment, you can have a walk on the beach in a moment." With trembling fingers he took coins out of his wallet. He held them on the palm of his hand, looked at them. He wouldn't need that many.

He put a gulden into the slot, slowly dialled the number of the weekend house. He got through at once. He stood there, looking out at the narrow uneven quay, the canal, the shining windowpanes beyond the humpbacked bridge and listened to the ringing tone. He was expecting that music again, but he heard only the ringing tone. A girl came over the top of the bridge on her bike, the top of her body swaying slowly back and forth.

After a minute the connection was automatically cut and switched to the engaged tone. Scholten replaced the receiver. He and his basket were already halfway out of the phone box – he had forgotten the gulden – when he hesitated.

He forced himself to go back into the phone box. He was about to look for another gulden, shook his head, retrieved the first, put it in the slot again, dialled the number once more.

When the connection was automatically cut for the second time, Scholten immediately picked up the basket and went to his car. He put the basket in it. "There, Manny, off we go now, it won't take long, three-quarters of an hour maybe, and then you'll see how nice it is at the seaside in Holland. You're really going to like it!"

At eleven Scholten reached the beach promenade. He carried the cat down to the beach, put it on the leash and took it for a walk. The cat retreated from the surf, stopped, crouched down, the tip of its tail twitched. When the water flowed back it stood up again, stretched its head, raised one paw. It retreated again when the surf next rolled in.

After a few hundred yards Scholten took off his shoes and socks, tied the shoes together by their laces, stuffed his socks in them, hung the shoes over his shoulder. He rolled up his trouser-legs. The sand was cold, but after he had run a little way, with the cat leaping about after him, his feet warmed up. He walked quite a long way north up the beach.

He met only a few people. They laughed, stopped, pointed at the cat. Once Scholten stopped too and let a little boy play with the cat for a while, until the child's parents called him and walked on with him. The boy kept turning round to look back.

The sky was cloudless, the foam of the waves coming in white as snow, sparkling as they broke and then flowed back. Scholten saw a steamer and three cutters out at sea. Now and then he carried the cat for a while, holding it in both arms and keeping it warm. "Well, little Manny, how about this, then? Did I promise you too much?" He sang now and then. "If all the water in the Rhine, if only it was golden wine". He broke off. He sang "Where the North Sea waves break, break upon the sand".

Halfway to the nearest village he climbed the wooden steps up the dunes. They set off pale horrible ideas in his mind, ideas that he immediately suppressed. His face twisted, but only for a moment. He went back through the wood on the dunes. He walked slowly, stopping often, letting the cat explore the rough grass by the side of the path.

At quarter to one he was sitting on the glazed veranda of a café on the beach promenade. He ordered a beer and a genever. He liked the waitress very much.

She spoke good German. She was medium height and sturdy, perhaps in her mid-forties. Could be a bit younger. Thick brown hair cut short. It clustered close to her head, as if it had been painted on. Brown eyes, quite large. He looked at her throat when she put the beer and genever down in front of him. A little lined already, like her chin. But she wasn't skinny.

Scholten ordered the soup of the day, sole with all the trimmings and an ice cream with chocolate sauce. When the waitress walked away he watched her go. My word, he thought, what legs.

She came back and brought the cat some raw meat cut up small on a plate and a cup of milk. Scholten said that wasn't necessary. She said oh, it was only leftovers. And she loved animals, particularly cats. Scholten asked if she had a cat herself. No, she'd had a cat once, but not now.

She asked if he was on holiday.

Scholten said yes.

She said well, he'd chosen a good time. It was dreadful here in summer, such crowds of people. Scholten said ah yes, the Germans. She said she had nothing against Germans. Far from it.

Scholten felt pleasantly touched but didn't know just what to reply. He smiled and said: "Ah, well." Then he said he was in luck, then.

She laughed and asked how long he was staying.

Scholten said he didn't know yet.

She said: "Oh." Then she asked if he was a *rentenier*. Scholten didn't quite understand, he was afraid she took him for an old age pensioner: in German a *Rentner*. She explained that she didn't know what the word was in German, but in Dutch it meant someone living on his own income. Oh, now he understood, said Scholten; he laughed, no, no, he hadn't reached those dizzy heights yet, he was afraid he still had to work.

He was in civil engineering, said Scholten. Road building and so on. Road building, she said, that must be a profitable business. Scholten said yes, but unfortunately not so profitable these days. The national debt, she'd understand, they were making economies everywhere, and firms like his bore the brunt of it. The waitress nodded.

When she brought his main course he asked her name. She said she was Frau Pattenier. Anna Pattenier. Scholten rose and said: "My name is Jupp Scholten." She smiled at him, opening her full lips and showing her teeth, a bright gold tooth among them, and said: "Pleased to meet you, Herr Scholten. Enjoy your lunch."

When Scholten had finished his ice cream and hot chocolate sauce he felt like an afternoon nap. He looked for the waitress. My goodness, if only I could take her to bed now. And then get up late in the afternoon, go for a little walk along the beach and through the woods then find a bar, have a couple of beers and something good to eat.

He looked at the time. Hell, past two already.

He took out his wallet, counted the notes. He called: "Frau Pattenier!" He stroked the cat. The banks were closed, but he knew that you could pay by Eurocheque anywhere in Holland.

He ordered a coffee and a black cigar and gave her a large tip. She said: "Oh!" and "Thank you very much!" He asked if she would be here this evening. She sighed, nodded and said yes, she was afraid so. And tomorrow too, right through Sunday. He asked if her husband didn't mind. She laughed and said it was nothing to do with him. Scholten said: "Oh

185

ho!" She stroked the cat and told him she was divorced.

Scholten got into his car. He put the cigar between his lips and puffed at it. He opened the window slightly and looked at the glazed veranda of the café. He couldn't see anything; the glass threw reflections back.

He started the car and drove off, but not out on the country road. He drove aimlessly through the village. At the northern end, where the last houses gave way to the dunes, he stopped. The mini-golf course lay deserted, its little flags blowing in the wind. The weather was warm and sunny.

Two-thirty. He could easily do it. Well, not exactly easily. He felt tired. Four beers and three genevers. So what? It was a long time since he'd been able to indulge himself like that. The booze tastes particularly good at lunch.

He wound the window down. It was very quiet. The wind blew over the dunes, the grasses moved soundlessly. Scholten looked up at the blue sky. He could really do with an afternoon nap.

An image took powerful hold of him: to stretch out between cool white sheets, one of those Dutch woollen blankets over him, a little window partly open, its two halves folding out and fastened to hooks, the curtain swaying in the wind now and then. And then Anna Pattenier comes in, gets undressed, stands there barefoot, moves, the floorboards creak, she pulls her panties down over her white buttocks, gets into bed, the mattress sags.

Scholten said: "Bloody hell." He took the cigar out of his mouth, looked at it, knocked the ash out of the window.

Who said he had to imitate Wallmann in every detail? Why did he necessarily have to be back at the house at six, just like Wallmann? And everything had gone all right. It didn't matter whether they began the search tomorrow morning or not until Monday. He had his alibi, and it wouldn't do any harm if he could prove it for an extra day either.

But suppose they asked how he could have stayed away so long without at least telling Hilde?

Well, what about it? He'd kept trying to call. The first time at the filling station on Friday. When she didn't answer he had thought she'd gone out and was looking for him down by the boat. Later, at the border crossing, he had thought she must already be asleep. And on Saturday morning he'd thought she simply wasn't answering the phone out of pure rage and venom. Was that so improbable? You don't know my wife, Superintendent. You don't know what she's like.

But staying away for two days just because of a quarrel? A quarrel? You must be joking! She'd made his life hell for him. Pure hell, all the time. And she'd hit the cat with a shoe on Friday evening. He was at his wit's end. Grandmontagne will bear me out, Superintendent.

Scholten started the car and drove slowly on. The first house he passed had a notice in the window: *Bed and Breakfast – Room Vacant.* An old woman stood in the front garden, bent over, pulling up a weed from the flowerbeds now and then.

Scholten took the room. It cost twenty-five gulden with breakfast, and she wouldn't charge any extra for milk for the cat, said the old lady.

As he undressed and hung his trousers over the chair under the sloping ceiling, he suddenly felt hot. He stopped. The strips of wood. And the insulating tape.

Wallmann had been able to burn the stuff on the

Friday evening. He hadn't. He'd had to put it off because Hilde didn't want him to light the fire. He'd meant to do it this evening, as soon as he got back and before calling the local policeman.

He stood there for a while in shirt and underpants. He was finding it difficult to think; drowsiness kept overcoming him, filling his brain with warmth. After a few moments he dismissed the idea. Nonsense.

They wouldn't search the house and the garage while there was no one there with a key. Grandmontagne would say Scholten had gone off to Holland, angry over the way his old lady nagged him. And Wallmann was in the Bahamas.

And even if they did, who was to say they'd notice anything odd about the strips of wood and the insulating tape? Well, yes, the nails were still in the strips of wood, he hadn't had a chance to knock them out again. But who'd ever notice that? Who would think up an idea like that?

He laughed. Who but Jupp Scholten would think up an idea like that? He unbuttoned his shirt.

And anyway, who was to say the body had already been found? Erika hadn't been found until the Sunday evening. And they'd been actively looking for her.

Scholten got between the sheets. The cat jumped up on the end of the bed, turned round a few times and then settled down.

He lay on his back, looking out of the window. The sky was blue. The curtain swayed in the wind now and then. After a while Scholten closed his eyes. He dreamed of Anna Pattenier. The real world in which he lived sank away. The world he wanted to live in welcomed him. It embraced him, it wrapped its arms and legs around him, it made a warm bed for him.

24

When he woke up twilight was falling. Scholten jumped up, got dressed, put the cat in the basket and drove into the village. One of the large general stores was open. He bought a shaver, shaving cream, eau de cologne, soap, a comb, a toothbrush and toothpaste. He even found a shirt his size and chose a tie to go with it. The shirt was dark brown with a thin yellow stripe. He'd never had one like it.

He drove back to the old woman's house and showered, washed his old shirt and hung it up. At seven-thirty he was back in the café on the beach promenade.

Anna Pattenier had her hands full with a coach-load of English tourists, women and a few men, evidently good business. Anna Pattenier spoke English to them, a language Scholten didn't understand.

He tried to get to know her better, and she was friendly to both him and the cat, but it was no use. She was very busy. A crowd of Dutch came in at nine-thirty too, and Anna Pattenier was on her feet all the time. At some point, when she brought him a fresh beer and another genever, she groaned and said she'd be falling into bed dead tired after this, what a day, no one had expected so many guests, and she had to be out here early tomorrow too.

By eleven Scholten was drunk. He paid, she asked if he'd be back tomorrow when she hoped she'd have more time. He said yes, he certainly would, picked up the basket and walked out of the door, holding himself very upright.

He missed the second step down from the veranda, stumbled, tried to save himself as he did so, slid over the pavement, landed in the road on one knee and one hand. The basket bounced on the road surface, the cat hissed.

Scholten said: "Hush, hush, little Manny, these things happen, don't be so touchy!" He got up, looked back to see if anyone had noticed his mishap.

The glass of the veranda was all steamed up. He dusted down his trousers, looked at his hand, which was slightly grazed.

He felt his way along the garden fence for the last few feet of his walk back to the house, breathing heavily. He peed against the fence, holding his penis with one hand.

After several unsuccessful attempts, he found the keyhole. He crawled up the steep stairs to his room flat on his front, so as not to run any risks, holding the basket up in the air with one hand. He just managed to hang his new shirt on one of the coat hangers and put his trousers over the chair. Then he fell heavily into bed.

After breakfast on Sunday morning he went to church. There was no Catholic service, so Scholten went to the Gereformeerde Kerk. The bare church and the plain liturgy left him cold for a long time; he looked around for Anna Pattenier, didn't see her, let his thoughts wander, sank back into the dream of his afternoon sleep the day before.

But at some point during one of the solemn, hoarsely sung hymns it caught up with him after all. Tears came into his eyes, he bowed his head, his shoulders shook. What he had done descended on him like a huge heavy weight, threatening to press him into the ground. He felt it at his throat, on his chest, on his back.

His lips moved, he spoke silently in despair and remorse. "Hilde, Hilde, forgive me, what have I done, dear God, forgive me, I must have been mad, I didn't know what I was doing." Fear shook him, hot and cold shivers ran down his back. Tears fell on his clasped hands.

He saw Hilde before him, fallen from the steps, grazed all over. Head injuries, yes, and some broken bones, and then lying in the water of the lake for almost two days. He put both hands over his face. Pity tormented him, compunction, remorse, yes, and a deep sense of horror. "What have I done?"

He did not calm down again until the end of the service. Composed now, he said several Our Fathers and Hail Marys, dedicating them to Hilde. Only when the congregation was leaving the church did he conclude his prayer. He prayed: "Dear God, don't forsake me. Save me. And give her poor soul eternal peace. Amen. And save me. Amen."

Walking slowly, head bent, he went back. He fetched the cat from his room, put it on its leash and walked up and down outside the house with it. After the cat had done its business he took it upstairs again. He wanted to be alone now, all alone.

He climbed up the dune and was going to climb down to the beach but hesitated. He looked round. Then he went back to the house. "The poor animal can't help it." He fetched the cat and took it for a walk along the beach and through the dunes.

At twelve-thirty he went into the café on the beach promenade with his basket. He had decided it would be better to have lunch before starting to drive back.

Anna Pattenier was not as busy as the evening before. She even sat down at Scholten's table with him for a moment. She did not get up until the landlady called to her from the kitchen. "Anneke!" He watched her walk away.

Later she came back and stood by him for a while. She folded her arms under her breasts and leaned against the side of the table, which pressed into her thigh.

Scholten cut a piece off his rump steak and said her job must be very stressful. She said yes, it was, but very interesting too with all the different guests, and it was all right today and probably wouldn't be so bad this evening, Sundays were never very busy. And tomorrow was her day off.

Scholten chewed, nodded, said: "Wonderful." He swallowed and asked what she did on her day off. She said tomorrow morning she'd be going into Amsterdam, she wanted to do some shopping, but she hoped to be back by the afternoon, and then she'd lie in the bathtub, have a really good bubble bath, lots and lots of bubbles, she always did that on her day off, and then she'd spoil herself, she usually didn't even get dressed again after her bath, she just lounged around in her dressing gown, didn't go out of doors, and in the evening she read for a bit or watched television.

Scholten nodded, cut another piece off the steak and asked when she was going to Amsterdam in the morning. She said, well, unfortunately rather early, she had to get the nine o'clock bus at the latest or it was so crowded, and she didn't like that.

Scholten chewed, nodded. He piled lettuce on his fork. He was about to convey the fork to his mouth, then stopped and put it down.

Coming to a sudden decision, he dismissed all the

irksome, worrying, frightening ideas lying in wait behind him. He said if she liked he could give her a lift to Amsterdam in his car.

She said: "Oh." And then she said oh, but she couldn't accept. Scholten said of course she could accept; he'd like to give her a lift. She asked if he had business in Amsterdam himself. He said not exactly, but that made no difference. He smiled. He said: "I'm a free man, after all. No one can tell me what to do, understand?"

She said she'd have to think it over, decide whether she could accept. He said there was nothing to think over, he was happy to do it, and if she liked he'd go shopping with her, or wait while she did her shopping, and then he could give her a lift back too.

She said no, no, he really mustn't. And what had she done to deserve it?

Scholten looked up from his plate. He smiled and said: "I like you."

She laughed, turned her head half away, looked sideways at him. "Herr Scholten, I think you are a great Casanova!" she said in Dutch.

Scholten laughed, raised his glass and took a long draught of beer, looked at her over the rim of the glass.

She came back to his table a couple more times. They agreed that he would pick her up at the entrance to the side street where she lived at quarter past nine. He left the café at three, slightly drunk.

He went back to his room. Lay on the bed. He refused to think about all the things he must do to avert trouble and all possible complications. After ten minutes he fell asleep, relaxed.

He got up at six, took the cat for a long walk, went to the café for supper at seven-thirty. Anna Pattenier was busy, but that didn't trouble him. He watched her

193

walking up and down, paid her compliments when she came over to his table. She came over quite often.

She came even when his glass was still full.

When he felt ready for bed he paid and left. He took the cat for another little walk. There was a clear starry sky above the dunes, but in the west a few silvery wisps of mist rose over the sea.

In the dark room, the sinister thing made its way up to him again. Scholten tossed and turned, plumped up the pillow, mopped the sweat from his brow. After a while he leaned over to the end of the bed, picked up the cat and cuddled it. He fell asleep to the sound of its purring.

25

He got up in good time on Monday morning. After breakfast he took the cat out. Half an hour later he brought it back to the room. He put it down on the bed, turned back again. The cat was standing there looking at him, waving its tail. He whispered: "I'll be back soon, Manny, you can't come with me now, be a good boy, I'll be back soon, understand?" The cat mewed and jumped off the bed. He quickly closed the door.

He looked at his watch. Eight-thirty. He climbed downstairs and knocked at the living-room door. The old lady was sitting in an armchair doing crochet. He asked if he could make a phone call to Germany; he'd give her three gulden, it wouldn't take long. The old lady nodded. "Yes, yes, *goed, goed.*"

He dialled the firm's office number. He had to dial it three times before he got through. Rosa Thelen answered. He said: "Rosie? Hello, Rosie. I can't come in to work today."

Rosa cried: "For heaven's sake, Herr Scholten, where are you? We've been so worried. We called your home, and no one answered, and then we called Herr Wallmann's weekend house, and no one answered there either. Where are you?"

"In Holland."

"Where? Holland? What are you doing there?"

"It happened all of a sudden. Listen, Rosie, I can't talk very long, it's a bit difficult." He cleared his throat. "I'm not at all well. I was taken ill here yesterday."

"For goodness' sake, what's the matter with you?"

"It's my heart and my circulation and so on. But I'm beginning to feel better. I think I'll be able to come home tomorrow, but I can't make it today. Tell Büttgenbach, would you?"

"Yes, of course."

"Right, Rosie, then . . ."

"Wait a moment, Herr Scholten, wait a moment! Tell me the address, so at least we know where you are."

Scholten hesitated.

Rosa said: "Herr Scholten? Where are you?"

He said: "In Heemswijk."

"What?"

"Heemswijk. Everyone here knows it. Not far from Amsterdam."

"And your address?"

"I'm not sure of the address exactly."

"Then at least tell me the phone number."

Scholten broke out in a sweat.

Rosa said: "We must be able to get in touch and make sure you're all right."

He read out the phone number.

Rosa said: "Right, I've got that."

Scholten said: "I must ring off, Rosie. And the doctor said I wasn't to get up again today. I only got out of bed to phone you."

"Well, you go right back to bed again. I'll tell Herr Büttgenbach at once."

"See you, Rosie."

"Herr Scholten! Just a moment. What about your wife? Is she at least all right so that she can look after you?"

"Yes, yes, everything's okay. See you, Rosie."

"See you, Herr Scholten! Look after yourself!"

Scholten hung up. He mopped the sweat from his brow. The old woman was looking at him with interest.

Scholten said: "Listen, Granny. Me ill. *Verstaan?* I go to bed."

The old lady looked at him, silently moving her lips.

Scholten said: "Listen. I ill." He pointed to his breast with his finger, then placed one hand on his forehead, the other on his heart and moaned. "I in bed." He put both hands together, laid his head sideways on them. "No phone." He shook his head, made a vigorous gesture of rejection. "No phone!"

The old lady nodded, moved her lips intently. Suddenly she burst into loud laughter. "Ah, yes, yes, I understand!" she said in Dutch. "You're sick! I understand. No phone!" She laughed again and nodded. "Yes, yes!"

Relieved, Scholten took out his wallet, gave her a five-gulden note, said: "That's right, thank you, Granny. *Dank u wel.*"

"*Alstublieft, meneer.*" She laughed and nodded.

Scholten went to the bank. He made out a cheque for three hundred marks and exchanged them for gulden. At ten past nine he parked opposite the side street. Five minutes later he saw Anna Pattenier walking down the street with a firm tread. She was wearing boots that fitted her calves snugly and a coat with a little fur collar. Scholten's heart beat faster.

Amsterdam was fresh and clean. Scholten navigated his way through the crowds of people in the shopping centre at Anna Pattenier's side, walking very upright, his head held high. He cracked jokes. Once Anna stopped and shook with laughter.

They went into three department stores, two pharmacists, a perfumery and three boutiques. Around eleven he bought her a bottle of scent in the perfumery. It was one she had pushed away because it was too expensive for her. She didn't want to accept it, but he told the salesgirl to pack it up and paid in cash.

Around one o'clock he wrote a cheque for 268 gulden in the last boutique. Anna had tried several dresses on, he had sat on a small curved chair outside the changing room, casting a sideways glance at it now and then, as if by chance. Through the gap beside the curtain he had seen her bare shoulder, and it looked as if she were wearing a black bra.

He had been asked what he thought about the dresses she tried on, and he had said he thought the green one suited her best. Anna was pleased, because she liked the green one best too, but she hadn't been quite sure whether it looked good on her.

Scholten rose from his chair while the salesgirl was hanging the other dresses up, went over to Anna and asked in a low voice if he could pay for the dress, he'd like to give it to her as a present. Anna said no, no, no, no, absolutely out of the question, she gestured with both hands and shook her head, but he wasn't giving way, after all, the salesgirl was standing there with the dress over her arm, smiling, and then Anna gave in, she said all right, but she must buy him a present too.

Out in the street Anna suddenly stopped, took hold of both his ears, kissed him on the mouth and said: "*Jupp, je bent een schat!*"

"I'm a what? A cat?"

She was convulsed with laughter. "No, no, not a cat. *Een schat*! A treasure, it means, a darling."

Scholten felt happy. He asked if he could call her Anneke. She wondered how he knew the name. He

said: "I heard the landlady in the café call you that."
She said only her friends could call her Anneke. And
the landlady. And Scholten.

Scholten said it was about time for a good lunch. She
said no, no, no, not yet. She dragged him on, and soon
they were standing outside the window of a gentleman's outfitters. She pointed to a green pullover and
said it would suit him very well, and it went with her
dress too. Scholten said: "No, certainly not. Anyway, I
have plenty of pullovers."

She insisted. In the end she dragged him into the
shop and bought him a shirt, blue with a very thin
stripe. She found a tie to go with it. The tie was very
expensive, and so was the shirt. Scholten stood there in
happy silence as she paid. His eyes were moist.

She took his arm. As they left the shop, she asked:
"Jupp, are you married?"

Scholten said: "I'm a widower."

They ate in a good restaurant. After the soup
Scholten reached for Anneke's hand and stroked it.
She smiled at him.

They were back beside the sea at about four. The sky
had clouded over. Scholten parked opposite the side
street. He took Anna's packages and followed her. She
stopped outside the door of a little house with low
windows.

"Another cup of coffee? Or a cup of tea?"

"Coffee would be nice. And a schnapps if you have
any." She laughed. Still in her coat, she put the coffee
water on the gas, poured two glasses of schnapps. She
took off her coat, threw it over the sofa and dropped
into an armchair, stretching her legs.

Scholten looked around. "It's comfortable here."

"You like it?"

"Wonderful."

She put one leg over the other and began tugging at her boot.

"Here, let me do that," he said. She stretched the leg out to him. He took hold of the boot, pulled. He looked nervously at the window. A woman was walking down the street, almost within reach. The curtain left three-quarters of the window clear to anyone's view.

He said: "Can we do it when people outside can look in?"

She laughed. "You're only taking my boots off. That won't interest anyone."

He pulled at the boot again. When it was off, he put a hand on her foot and said: "But I'd like to do more."

Anna laughed. She sighed. "Jupp, we're too old for that sort of thing. And much too sensible."

"Too old, are we? Draw the curtain, and then I'll show you."

She laughed. "It's not the kind of curtain you can draw."

He took her second boot off, stood up, tried the curtain. "So it isn't." He looked at her. "Then let's go into the bedroom."

"I thought you were a nice man."

"I am. It's just because I'm so nice I'd like to go into the bedroom with you."

She laughed. "You stay here and drink your coffee and your schnapps while I put on something else." She stood up, took her boots and coat and went into the back room. She left the door ajar.

He clasped his hands between his knees, pressed them together, swayed his torso to and fro, smiling with delight. He had to stop himself shouting out loud for happiness. He took another sip of coffee. Then he stood up and went to the door of the back room. He knocked.

"Yes?"

"Can I come in?"

He heard her laugh. Then she sighed. "Jupp, what did I say to you? You must be sensible."

He gently opened the door.

"I am. It wouldn't be very sensible to stay in there drinking coffee."

Her feet were bare; she was holding a dressing gown in front of her breasts. He saw her naked shoulders, her hips, part of her thigh.

He said, his throat constricted: "Put that dressing gown down. Just for a moment."

She looked at him, shook her head. "Jupp, I'm not pretty. And I'm much too old."

"Don't talk such nonsense. You're a wonderful woman." He went over to her, placed his hands on her shoulders. Her skin was smooth and cool. He swallowed. "You're driving me crazy." He drew her towards him.

She held the dressing gown tight in both hands. She put her head on his shoulder. He heard her breathing faster and deeper. His excitement grew. He ran his hands over her bare back.

She said, into the hollow of his throat: "Does it always have to be so quick?"

"How do you mean, quick? Life is short. Who knows how much longer we have to live?" He massaged her back, tried to bring his hands forward and get at her breasts. She pressed the dressing gown to her body.

He said in a voice that he hardly recognized as his own: "What are you doing?" He cleared his throat. "Do you want to drive me even crazier?"

She raised her head from his shoulder and looked at him. "Why don't you even give me a kiss?"

He kissed her. A sound escaped his throat as he felt her return the kiss, tenderly, very carefully.

He put his fingers inside her panties, took her bottom in both hands and pressed it to him, beginning to move his lower body.

She removed her lips from his, laid her face against his throat again. Her breathing was heavy.

He suddenly felt and heard her sobbing against his shoulder. He said in a strangely small, hoarse voice, "What's the matter?" He went on moving his lower body, trying to get one of his hands round to the front of the panties.

When she sobbed again, violently, he stopped. He leaned his head and chest back and looked at her. "What is it?"

Her face was wet with tears.

He swallowed. "What's the matter?" He was upset himself, wondering how he could overcome this setback. "What have I done wrong?" He ran his fingertips over her cheeks, wiping the tears away.

She freed herself from his arms, let the dressing gown fall, went barefoot to the bed and sat down. She sat there, her shoulders drooping, her heavy breasts resting on the curve of her stomach. She wept.

He went over to her, put out a hand to take hold of one breast and then the other, lifted them a little way, felt them. He stroked her back with his other hand. "What's the matter? Do stop crying. It's nothing to cry about. It's good."

He stroked her belly. Then he put his hand inside the panties and brought his fingers round to the front. She didn't resist. She sat there motionless, tears running down her cheeks. He tried to spread her legs.

Suddenly she raised her eyes and looked at him through her tears. She said: "You only gave me the dress because you wanted to go to bed with me. And the perfume."

"What are you talking about?" His hand went on working away. "What makes you think that? You're not a tart."

"But you think I am."

"Me? What makes you think so?" He felt her yielding. She spread her legs a little. He said: "Oh yes, that's good. You're a wonderful woman."

"I'm a tart, that's what you think I am." She dropped back on the bed, closed her eyes. "Take the dress, Jupp, and the perfume. I don't want them."

His hand froze.

She put both arms over her face. She said: "You only wanted to go to bed with me. It's always the same."

He was breathing heavily. He shook his head.

Suddenly he lay down beside her. He took her in both arms. He said: "That's absolutely wrong. What makes you think such a thing? I didn't give you the dress because I wanted to go to bed with you. Or the perfume. I gave them to you because I thought you'd be pleased. That's all. If you don't want . . . if you don't want to do anything now, then we needn't. We have plenty of time. I thought you wanted to. There's no point in it unless we both want to. Or I wouldn't enjoy it myself. We have plenty of time, Anneke." He rocked her a little in his arms. "Anneke. We have plenty of time. Come on, Anneke. Do stop crying. Come on, Anneke. I won't do anything to you."

They lay there on the bed for a while, legs dangling over the edge. He stroked her arms, her hair. She put an arm round him, drew him close. He said: "Yes, yes, I'm here. I'll stay with you, Anneke. You don't have to be afraid. I won't do anything to you."

She said: "Jupp."

He said: "There, there. And no more waitressing. You shouldn't work so hard. We'll talk about it. You ought to have a good life. Everything will be different from now on. You wait and see, Anneke."

She held him close.

He said: "There, there."

He felt his right leg going numb. "Anneke, I'll have to stand up for a minute," he said. "My leg's gone to sleep."

She laughed. She let go of him. He stood up and placed his foot carefully on the floor. She sat up, wiped the tears from her eyes, pointed at the leg. "This one?"

"Yes." He swung the leg. "Damn it, it feels like a thousand pins and needles."

She reached for the leg, massaged it with both hands. He moaned, uttered a suppressed cry. She stopped, looked at him. "Not good?"

"Yes, yes, it's very good. Go on. It's just, oh, damn it, it tickles so much." He began chuckling.

In the end they were both laughing out loud. He picked her up from the bed and they stood with their arms round each other. He felt her breasts on his chest.

After a while he sighed. He wiped the tears from his eyes, took her by the shoulders, looked at her and said: "Listen, Anneke. You have your bubble bath now. And have a little rest too. And meanwhile I'll go and see to my cat. He'll want to go out, poor creature, he's been shut up in the room since morning. Then I'll come back with the cat. It won't take long, don't worry."

She looked at him very gravely.

He felt cold, his heart began to thud. "Or would you rather I didn't come back?"

She said: "You idiot. Go on, be quick, and then come back quick with your cat."

204

Scholten did not take his car. He had a great need to feel the wind on his face and the sprinkling of raindrops falling from the dark grey sky.

Twilight was coming on. He walked down the village street, past the warm light of the shop windows, the glowing doorways of bars.

A hundred thousand marks. He'd take over one of those bars. If not in Heemswijk, somewhere else. There were hundreds of such bars in the seaside villages, thousands of them.

Anna knew about the business. She'd be tops in gastronomy. And he'd provide the money and keep the books. That would suit him, he was a trained bookkeeper after all. A bar like that would be child's play compared to the firm of Ferd. Köttgen, Civil Engineering Contractors. And he knew the way Köttgen operated inside out.

Anna would do the shopping. No, she'd make a list of what they needed, and he would drive off and get it all in the morning. And in the evening, when they'd closed the door behind the last guests, they'd sit together at the cash desk counting the takings, and he'd write everything down, and they'd have a little drink, a beer and a genever for him, maybe a sherry for Anna, and they'd think about what there was to be done next day.

The wind blows around the house, sometimes howls around the house, shakes the shutters in autumn and spring. It makes the house shake in winter when the sea rolls in like thunder under the dark night sky, trying to catch the dunes in its drift of foam and then withdrawing with a roar into the black night.

They'll count the money and lock it in the safe, and then they'll climb the stairs and go into their bedroom, the central heating has warmed it up, it's as comfortable as being back in the womb, the wind leaps up at the little windowpanes but it always falls back powerless, it can't do them any harm.

They get undressed, Anna stands there barefoot, she takes her panties off, she bends down, her white buttocks are taut, she raises her leg and pulls the panties over her foot. She puts her nightie over her head, she stretches her arms, the nightie falls over her buttocks, and then she comes to him, the mattress sinks, come here, Anna, my Anneke, she embraces him, warmth, warmth, the white cushion of her breasts, her belly, she flings one leg over him, draws him close to her, Anneke, my Anneke, her lips are soft and moist.

26

When Scholten put his key in the lock the door was suddenly opened. The old lady stood there. She was nodding excitedly and speaking in Dutch. He could just about follow her.

"*Meneer*, two gentlemen were asking for you. One from Germany and the other is a Dutchman."

"What's up?"

She waved both hands. "Two gentlemen." She raised two fingers then dug her forefinger into his chest. "They want to talk to you. It's urgent."

"Wait a moment." He raised two fingers himself to make sure he had understood. "Two gentlemen?"

She nodded. "Yes, yes."

"And they want to talk to me?"

"Yes, yes, they're waiting for you in the café on the beach promenade."

"Café? Beach promenade?"

"Yes, yes, they said it's urgent."

Scholten stared at the old lady. She was nodding excitedly. He said: "What do they want?"

"They're waiting in the café on the beach promenade."

"Yes, I get that bit." He looked down the road, and then at the old lady. "Were they from the firm of Köttgen? Did they say Köttgen? Köttgen, *verstaan*? From Germany?"

She nodded. "Yes, one was from Germany. And the other is Dutch. They're sitting in the café."

"Yes, right, I'll go and find them." He passed her, climbed the stairs. She watched him.

He gulped his fears down. He called: "Manny? I'm back. Where's my boy?"

He carefully opened the door, looked down at the floor. "Now we're going for a walk, little Manny."

The crack in the doorway was empty. Scholten opened the door fully, went into the room. The cat was nowhere to be seen. He bent down, looked under the bed, straightened up, felt the bedspread. His glance fell on the window. He had forgotten to close it. Both halves were open, fastened to their hooks. The damp wind lifted the little curtains.

"Oh, bloody hell!" He went to the window, looked out. The sloping roof of the shed was right below the window. "Manny?" He made coaxing noises, whistled a long, shrill note. "Where are you? Come home at once. Come here, little Manny. Come on, boy, we're going for a walk."

Suddenly he closed the window. Then he opened it again and fastened the hooks again. He picked up the basket and leash and hurried downstairs. The old lady was still standing in the corridor. She looked at him, her lips moving silently.

"Have you seen my cat? *Kat, verstaan?*" He mewed.

"*Uw kat?*" She shook her head; no, she had not seen his cat.

He went out into the road, whistled, smacked his lips. He looked in the front garden. "Manny?"

He stopped. Perhaps the cat had run off into the dunes. Perhaps it had run into the woods.

He was going to turn and go along the path to the woods on the dunes when he remembered the two gentlemen in the café. Bloody hell. Sweat broke out on him. He hurried along the road to the beach promenade, looking into every yard he passed. "Manny?"

There were not many people in the café. A young girl in a black dress and white apron was leaning against the bar, her legs crossed. Two men were sitting at the table in the corner of the glazed veranda. Scholten didn't know them. One rose and came towards him. "Herr Scholten?"

"Yes?"

"Ah, wonderful! We thought you'd never turn up. My name is Maubach." He offered his broad hand with a smile. Scholten took the hand. "Pleased to meet you." He swallowed. "What's this about?"

"I'll explain. Can we talk for a moment?" Maubach pointed to the corner table.

"Well, yes. It's just that I'm in rather a hurry."

"I don't think this will take long. It really would be very helpful if you could spare us a few minutes." Maubach led him to the corner and indicated the other man. "This is Herr Huygens. And this is Herr Scholten, who is so much in demand."

Huygens laughed, stood up and shook hands with Scholten. Scholten sat down. He was feeling a little better. If only the cat would come back.

The girl came over. Maubach asked Scholten what he would like to drink. Scholten asked for a beer and a genever.

Maubach rubbed his hands, looked at Scholten and said: "Herr Scholten, we need your help."

"My help? What with?"

"You'll understand in a moment. I am a chief super-intendent in the CID, and Herr Huygens is from the Amsterdam CID."

Scholten rubbed his ear. "CID? What do I have to do with the CID?"

Maubach laughed. "Don't be alarmed, Herr Scholten. And I must apologize for taking you by surprise like this, but we're in rather a hurry." He looked at Scholten. "I called your home this morning, but there was no answer. And then I called your office and was told you were here, and that you weren't well. The lady I spoke to said they didn't know when you would be back, and you had to stay in bed."

Scholten said: "Yes, well, when I rang this morning I was still feeling rather rough. I didn't expect to be up and about again so soon myself."

"No need to explain, Herr Scholten." Maubach laughed. "These things happen. You can feel terrible, and then you're much better all of a sudden."

Huygens said: "It's the sea air. It could bring the dead back to life." He laughed. Maubach agreed, "Yes, you've got it good out here. I wouldn't mind being unwell in Heemswijk myself." He waited until the girl had brought the drinks.

"Well, it's like this, Herr Scholten. There is some urgency about this business, and we can't get any further without a statement from you. So I got into my car and drove over the border. And my colleagues in Amsterdam were kind enough to say they had no objection to my asking you a few questions here and now. Beside your sickbed." He laughed, raised his glass, drank first to Huygens and then to Scholten.

He wiped his lips, examined the glass. "Herr Scholten, I'll be frank with you. However, I must ask you to be discreet. You mustn't talk to anyone else about this. Can I trust you?"

"Of course. Of course. But I don't know what you're talking about."

Maubach looked at him. "Herr Scholten, we strongly suspect that Frau Wallmann's death was not an accident. And we have always had grave doubts of the theory that she *voluntarily* jumped off the steps."

Scholten's heart began to thud. He stared at Maubach. "What do you mean?"

"Murder, Herr Scholten. We think Frau Wallmann was murdered."

"Murder?" Scholten's voice was thin; it sounded strange to him. He cleared his throat. "But who would have murdered her?"

"Think about it, Herr Scholten. You know the situation in the Köttgen company. You know more about it than anyone else, or so Herr Büttgenbach told me, anyway, and he should know."

Scholten nodded. "Yes, yes. I mean, who do you think did it?" He looked at Maubach. "You don't mean . . . ?"

Maubach nodded. "Of course. Herr Wallmann. That can't surprise you too much, Herr Scholten. Look around you. Of all the people with whom Frau Wallmann had dealings, who had a motive?"

Scholten looked out of the veranda. He was thinking feverishly.

The girl brought his beer. He reached for it and took a long draught without toasting the other two men. He wiped his mouth.

Maubach said: "Do you understand?"

Scholten cleared his throat. "But that's nonsense. That's just impossible. Herr Wallmann, I mean, he has an alibi. It can't have been him. It's a watertight alibi."

Maubach nodded. "I know. That's why we could get no further at the time. And that's why we had to close the file on the case and hand it back to the public prosecutor's office."

Scholten looked at him. "Then why now? I mean, why do you now think it was Wallmann?"

Maubach laughed. "Well, you see, Herr Scholten, sometimes the police aren't as useless as people think."

"Good for the police," said Huygens.

"You may well say so. One of my younger colleagues, Herr Scholten, he couldn't get the case out of his mind. He was convinced from the first that Herr Wallmann had thought up a very clever ruse. Yes, and then there was a strange anonymous phone call, someone called and said Herr Wallmann had murdered his wife. And that got my colleague looking into the case again. On the side, you understand, as well as his regular work. That's why it's taken rather a long time."

Scholten said: "When was this?"

"The anonymous call? Some time in May. Frau Wallmann was buried long before then." Maubach took a notebook out of his pocket, leafed through it. "It was May 12. A Monday. The caller said, 'Frau Erika Wallmann of the civil engineering firm of Ferdinand Köttgen didn't die in an accident. She was murdered. By her husband. You ought to investigate . . . ' And then he hung up. Yes, it was definitely rather odd."

Scholten said: "And you don't know who phoned?"

"No, it was impossible to trace the caller."

Scholten said: "But surely your colleague couldn't find out any more – I mean, Frau Wallmann had been dead for almost two months on May 12. There wouldn't be any evidence left."

"Yes, so you might think." Maubach looked at the time. "But my colleague went to look at those steps again last week. Up at the Wallmanns' weekend house by the lake."

"The steps?"

"Yes, last Monday. A week ago today. And he found some odd things." Maubach smiled. "Nail-holes in the

212

front edges of a couple of planks." He looked at Huygens. "Those steps are made of really good solid timber."

Huygens nodded.

Maubach said: "And the holes were very regularly spaced. Four of them, side by side. He found them on the landing where the steps turned a bend. And on the two steps above the landing. And nowhere else. Odd, don't you think?"

Scholten passed a hand over his face. His throat tightened. He swallowed. "But what's odd about that? The steps are ancient. They must be full of the marks of nails."

"Ah, but these nail-holes were quite new. And listen to this. My colleague took out one of the planks – and it came out quite easily. The bolts holding it in place had been greased. It had to have been done fairly recently. And then he found that these nail-holes were not just in the front edge of the plank but in all four edges."

Scholten could have groaned aloud. He cleared his throat. "So what? Like I said, they're full of nail-holes."

"Well, no, Herr Scholten. No, no. These are perfectly regular. Four holes in each of the long sides and two in each of the narrow sides. And now, listen to this. We sat down and tried to work out what it meant. Because at first sight there seemed no sense in it. But then the penny dropped."

"What penny?" Scholten took out his handkerchief and rubbed the nape of his neck. "What kind of penny dropped?"

"Keep listening. Back in March we'd already wondered how Frau Wallmann could have fallen down those steps. She was a strong healthy woman; she wasn't hobbling around on a stick. And even back then one of us said – it was just meant as a joke, you see – one of us said there must have been a sheet of black ice on the steps or she could never have fallen down them. We thought that was funny. We didn't understand the facts at the time, and they weren't obvious either. But that's exactly what it was: black ice." He looked at Huygens. "Murder by black ice."

Huygens shook his head. "Amazing. You did a good job there."

Scholten laughed. He thought it was someone else he heard laughing. "But that's nonsense," he said. "How could there be ice on the steps at the end of March? In fine spring weather?"

Maubach smiled. "Just suppose, Herr Scholten, you take out those planks and nail strips of wood to them all the way round. You let the strips come a little way above the planks, and you waterproof the whole thing, say with insulating tape. Do you know what you get then?"

"How would I know?"

"You get a kind of basin or dish, understand? And then you fill it with water, an inch or so deep, and you put it in a freezer. Guess what you have on that plank next morning?"

Huygens said: "Black ice." He shook his head. "Amazing. Unbelievable."

Maubach looked at Huygens. "Our colleagues in the TCI tried it. We wanted to make sure. And it really does work."

Scholten said: "Who tried it?"

"Sorry, TCI is our abbreviation. The Technical Criminal Investigation department."

"They can be wrong, I suppose."

Maubach laughed. "Not them, Herr Scholten. Not with something of this nature. They're wise to anything, they are."

"Maybe. But suppose Herr Wallmann simply says it isn't true. How are you going to prove it when he has an alibi?"

"Ah, don't you understand, Herr Scholten? He has an alibi for the time when his wife fell off the steps, yes. But the planks could have been prepared and fitted beforehand. That's the clever part of this ruse: he wasn't there when it happened, and by the time he came back and called the police the ice had long since melted. Now do you get it?"

"Get it? Of course I get it. But you still can't prove it. Even if it's true. You'll never be able to prove it."

"I wouldn't say 'never'. But it will be very difficult, I have to admit that you're right there. And that's why we're here. We need your help, Herr Scholten."

"My help?"

Scholten noticed that his voice sounded rough and cracked. He tried to suppress his despair again just for a minute, shake it off, feel free for one brief moment. "How could I help you? You don't think Herr Wallmann invited me to watch him, do you?"

"Of course not. But we're aware that you not only know your way around the firm, you're familiar with the house up there too. You've often done odd jobs in it. You've bought DIY materials for Herr Wallmann."

"So?"

Maubach said firmly: "Herr Scholten. Can you, for instance, remember thin wooden strips of any kind going missing up there? Or insulating tape? People often need such things in a house like that. Or did you find any remnants lying about? You were working up there for a few days at the end of April, something odd might have struck you. Of course it is clear to us that Herr Wallmann, if he did what we think he did, will have cleared away everything he used. He had plenty

215

of time. He could burn the wooden strips in the fire, for instance. But perhaps you can tell us about anything that was missing afterwards, Herr Scholten. You and only you can do it, I feel pretty sure. You're the one with the overall view."

Scholten stared out of the veranda. The lights on the beach promenade were switched on, and there was a black sky behind them. A very narrow, pale green streak on the horizon divided the sky from the black sea.

The strips of wood. He ought to have driven back on Saturday to burn them, and then he ought to have called the local policeman and reported her missing. Why hadn't he gone back on Saturday? He ought to have done everything exactly as Wallmann had.

They couldn't pin anything on Wallmann. He had burned the strips at once, after fitting the planks in place. Yes, but he couldn't have done that with Hilde. Wallmann had been alone in the house, but Hilde wouldn't have a fire in the hearth. "We're not having that fire lit."

Hilde. He'd always known she would be the death of him some day.

Maubach cleared his throat. He said: "If he did what we think he did, then he needed ten strips of wood measuring twenty-eight inches each, and ten measuring nine and a half inches each. Or a little longer. Strips around two inches wide. In all he'd have needed about ten or eleven yards of thin wooden strips. And probably the same amount of insulating tape, or some other waterproofing material, Herr Scholten. Is there anything like that missing from the house? Take your time, Herr Scholten. Think about it carefully."

Huygens said: "It's very important. That could be

conclusive evidence, you see. Our man can't be convicted without it."

Maubach said: "It is indeed very important, Herr Scholten. As you know, Herr Wallmann is in the Bahamas. I'll tell you something else to put you fully in the picture. I know you're a reliable and trustworthy man, and I can talk frankly to you."

He cleared his throat. "Over the past few months, Herr Wallmann has been transferring money abroad. Quite a lot of money. We suspect he's planning to leave the country some time. Perhaps by now he's beginning to doubt whether he really did commit the perfect murder. Perhaps he's scared and thinking of disappearing in the near future. And then he'll be gone, you understand? And heaven knows whether we'll ever be able to put him behind bars."

Scholten took a deep breath. He coughed, but the pressure did not lift from his chest. His eyes slid over Maubach, went from Maubach to Huygens. Then he looked out at the dark again.

Yes, that was it. That was about it. They couldn't pin anything on Wallmann. He had burned the strips and the insulating tape. And the ice had melted long ago. All of six months ago it had melted to water and evaporated in the sunlight and fallen again as rain – several times, perhaps. There was nothing now, nothing at all, they could pin on Wallmann. "What do you say about that, Herr Wallmann?" About what, pray? There was no evidence.

They would never get their hands on Wallmann.

Scholten took a deep breath. He looked at Huygens and then at Maubach. He said: "Can I make a phone call?"

"A phone call? Of course."

Scholten went up to the bar. He asked if he could

make a long-distance call to Germany. The landlady put the phone in front of him. He passed one hand over his face, stared at the dial then began to dial the number of the weekend house. The engaged signal interrupted him twice in the middle of the dialling code. On the third try he got through.

He stared at the bar counter. He listened impassively to the ringing tone. He had no hope left.

When the connection was automatically broken he pressed down the rest, held it there for a moment, took a deep breath, dialled the number of his apartment. The ringing tone came. He stood there as if with his mind on something else. He waited again until the ringing tone was automatically broken.

27

He went back to the table, sat down. Maubach and Huygens were looking at him intently.

Scholten said: "It was exactly the way you said. He did it with black ice. He used five wooden strips each measuring seven feet. And about ten yards of insulating tape. I know exactly what was in the house before. The wooden strips and the insulating tape were missing."

Maubach's voice suddenly sounded hoarse. "When? When you were up there in April?"

"Yes. I can tell you more too. He bought new bolts. He used them for the substitute planks."

"What do you mean, substitute planks?"

"There are half a dozen old planks up in the garage. I fitted new ones in the autumn. He put the old planks back in the stairs when he took out those five and put them in the freezer. Or someone might have noticed the hole in the flight of steps."

Maubach nodded, attending closely. "Of course."

"And I can tell you something about the alibi. He planned it ahead, in detail. He left those files in the office on purpose. He had locked them up so that no one could find them and Erika couldn't bring them with her for him. Or perhaps he secretly took them with him after all. He did it so that he could say he had to go back to town. And he got drunk on purpose at the bowling club. So Sauerborn would say he couldn't drive back to the house that evening."

Huygens said: "Fantastic. That'll get Herr Wallmann behind bars. Congratulations, Herr Maubach."

Scholten said: "And he fixed it all to make sure Erika went down the steps. The sailing trip. The mainsheet had jammed, he said – nonsense. He hit the tackle with a hammer so that he'd have to have a new one. I saw the bill from the yachting basin. Erika was supposed to think he was having difficulty getting his bit of fluff out of the place early enough. Fräulein Faust, I mean. The idea was for Erika to think she could catch him with Fräulein Faust. And she did think so too. She went down the steps, and then she fell. He killed her, the bastard."

Scholten's voice broke. He sobbed aloud, put a hand over his eyes and wept.

Maubach laid a hand on his back. He said: "There, there, Herr Scholten. We'll get him. And with your help I think we can convict him. I'm almost sure of it, in fact. Do calm down, Herr Scholten. I can understand you taking it so badly. You were a good friend of Frau Wallmann, weren't you?"

Scholten nodded, his hand over his eyes.

Maubach stood up. "Well, I must make some phone calls." He went to the bar.

Huygens said nothing. Not until Scholten leaned back and looked for his handkerchief did he say, "Herr Scholten, you have helped the police a great deal. If only everyone was like you we'd have an easier time. And the criminal fraternity would have a much worse one."

Scholten wiped the tears from his eyes, blew his nose.

Maubach came back. He said: "The wheels have started moving. I must set off. Thank you very much indeed, Herr Scholten." He offered his broad hand. "When will you be back?"

Scholten shrugged. "I don't know yet. Maybe tomorrow."

"Tomorrow would be good. Anyway, please call me as soon as you're home." Maubach handed him a card. "And mind how you drive. We'll be needing you again." He laughed. Huygens shook hands with Scholten and clapped him on the shoulder.

Scholten dropped back on his chair. He watched them leave through the glass of the veranda. The landlady came up to the table, stacked the empty glasses on a tray. "Anything else?"

Scholten stared at her then shook his head. "No, nothing more thank you. *Alstublieft. Dank u wel.*"

"*Alstublieft, meneer.*" She smiled. "Anneke will be in again tomorrow."

Scholten nodded. When she had already gone he said: "Yes, yes. *Dank u wel.*"

After a while he stood up. He bent ponderously, picked up the basket, made sure the cat's leash was still in it. He went out. There was no one to be seen in the pale light of the street lamps. The wind blew in restless gusts over the beach promenade, carrying moisture on it. Scholten could hear the breakers. He stopped and listened.

He went a few steps, stopped again. Suddenly he called: "Manny!" He listened. All he could hear was the breakers and the moaning of the wind.

He turned up his coat collar and hurried on. As he approached the house he ran. He heard the TV from the living room. He climbed the stairs, carefully opened the door, put one hand in and switched on the light. The cat wasn't there. The little curtains fluttered at the window.

He looked down at the yard, which was all dark, a few blurred outlines, a puddle shining. "Manny? Are you down there? Come up at once!" He listened. Then he went back, switched the light off, closed the door and went downstairs. He knocked at the living-room door.

"Come in!"

He looked in. The old lady was in her armchair in front of the TV set. Scholten said: "The cat?"

"The cat?" She shook her head, gestured with both hands. No, she hadn't seen the cat, she said; she'd looked for it but she hadn't found it. She began to get up.

"No, no, don't get up, Granny. I'll go and look. *Alstublieft.*"

He stopped outside the house. There were lights in the living-room windows of the little houses all around. The wind scattered a few raindrops on his forehead. He looked up at the sky. Black, not a star to be seen.

He called, "Manny! Come along now!" His voice dropped, he said: "This is much too cold for you. You'll fall sick on me if you run around in this. And it's beginning to rain – listen to me, will you?"

He listened. He heard something, he didn't know if it was the wind or just the blood racing in his ears. He went a few paces.

Suddenly fear and despair broke over him like a huge wave, unexpectedly rolling up. He stopped, held on to the garden fence. Head drawn in, chin on his chest, he waited for the wave to recede. He coughed.

He went on, at first tentatively, trying to find his way through the dark, then faster and faster. He turned off on the path leading into the wooded dunes. Now and then he stumbled, saved himself, went on without slowing his pace. Twigs whipped into his face. At regular intervals he called, "Manny! Little Manny!"

Sometimes he whistled too. He called once again,

"Come here, boy! I'm here! You don't need to go looking for me."

His heart took a mighty leap, relief and happiness ran through him when he felt a light touch against his shoes, his legs, something clinging to him and following him. He bent down. It was a twig that had blown off a bush. Tears came into his eyes.

He went on, tried to take his handkerchief out, gave up, wiped his eyes with the back of his hand. "Little Manny! Come along, do!"

Finally the path left the wood, wound up the slope of the dune through grasses and low bushes, went down to the beach on the other side.

Scholten stumbled down the slope through drifts of sand. His knees buckled, he recovered, staggered, climbed on down blindly in the darkness. He fell on his knees, propping himself on both hands as he kneeled there.

The sand was wet and cold. Scholten wiped his eyes with the back of his hand, tried to make something out through the veil of tears blurring them. That must be the sea over there; the surf breathed with a rumbling sound. He thought he could see the white border of foam shimmering in the dark.

A sob tightened his throat. He swallowed violently, coughed. Then he called, in a strange, thin, high voice: "Manny! Where are you, little boy? Why did you run away? Come back, do, little Manny!"

He bowed his head and gave himself up to tears. He kneeled there for a long time, his hands in the damp cold sand, weeping quietly. His shoulders shook only now and then. He said, his chin on his chest: "You'll be ill, little boy."

After a while he struggled up again. He tottered a few steps down the slope, stumbled and fell. He did not try to break this fall. He fell with his face in the sand.

He raised his head and said: "Manny. Dear boy. Come along now. Let's go home."

THUMBPRINT

Friedrich Glauser

"It's a fine example of the craft of detective writing in a period which some regard as the golden age of crime fiction." *The Sunday Telegraph*

"This genuine curiosity compares to the dank poetry of Simenon and reveals the enormous debt owed by Duerenmatt, Switzerland's most famous crime writer, for whom this should be seen as a template." *The Guardian*

The death of a travelling salesman in the forest of Gerzenstein appears to be an open and shut case. Studer is confronted with an obvious suspect and a confession to the murder. But nothing is what it seems. Envy, hatred, sexual abuse and the corrosive power of money lie just beneath the surface. Studer's investigation soon splinters the glassy façade of Switzerland's tidy villages, manicured forests and seemingly placid citizens. *Thumbprint*, a European crime classic, was first published in 1936.

Diagnosed a schizophrenic, addicted to morphine and opium, Friedrich Glauser spent the greater part of his life in psychiatric wards, insane asylums and prison. His elegant prose and acute observation conjure up a world of those at the margins of society.

"With this book alone, Bitter Lemon Press justifies its mission to bring out the best of European crime fiction. Slickly written and character driven, the novel is rooted in its Swiss environment, where malice and money meet." *Belfast Telegraph*

"A picture of Switzerland far different from that depicted in travel brochures. Throughout there is a brooding feeling and the characterisation is spot on. This first publication in English should ensure that Sergeant Studer becomes just as well known in the UK as he is on the Continent." *Eastern Daily Press*

£8.99/$13.95
Crime paperback original, ISBN 1–904738–800–1
www.bitterlemonpress.com

THE SNOWMAN

Jörg Fauser

"Prose that penetrates the reader's mind like speed, fast paced, without an ounce of fat." *Weltwoche*

Blum's found five pounds of top-quality Peruvian cocaine in a suitcase. His adventure started in Malta, where he was trying to sell porn magazines, the latest in a string of dodgy deals that never seem to come off. A left-luggage ticket from the Munich train station leads him to the cocaine. Now his problems begin in earnest. Pursued by the police and drug traffickers, the luckless Blum falls prey to the frenzied paranoia of the cocaine addict and dealer. His desperate and clumsy search for a buyer takes him from Munich to Frankfurt, and finally to Ostend. This is a fast-paced thriller written with acerbic humour, a hardboiled evocation of drug-fuelled existence and a penetrating observation of those at the edge of German society.

Jörg Fauser, born in Germany in 1944, was a novelist, essayist and journalist. Having broken his dependency on heroin at the age of thirty he spent much of the rest of his working life dependent on alcohol. He nevertheless produced three successful novels including *The Snowman*. On 16 July 1987 he had been out celebrating his forty-third birthday. At dawn, instead of going home, he wandered on to a stretch of motorway, by chance or by choice, and was struck down by a heavy-duty lorry. He died instantly.

"A wonderful crime novel. If justice prevailed Fauser would be world-famous overnight." *Frankfurt Allgemeine*

"Masterful portrayal of the enchantment and beauty hidden in the dark, dirty corners of life." *Südddeutshe Zeitung*

£8.99/$13.95
Crime paperback original, ISBN 1–904738–05–2
www.bitterlemonpress.com

TEQUILA BLUE

Rolo Diez

"Both a scathing and picaresque comedy, a biting and spicy concoction. Just like tequila." *Le Monde*

It's not easy being a cop in Mexico City.

Meet Carlos Hernandez, Carlito to his women. He's a police detective with a complicated life. A wife, a mistress, children by both and a pay-check that never seems to arrive. This being Mexico, he resorts to money laundering and arms dealing to finance his police activity. The money for justice must be found somewhere.

The corpse in the hotel room is that of a gringo with a weakness for blue movies. Carlito's maverick investigation leads him into a labyrinth of gang wars, murdered prostitutes and corrupt politicians.

A savagely funny, sexy crime adventure that is a biting satire of life in Mexico.

Rolo Diez, born in Argentina in 1940, was imprisoned for two years during the military dictatorship and forced into exile. He now lives in Mexico City, where he works as a novelist, screenwriter and journalist.

"Diez describes a country torn by corruption, political compromise, and ever-threatening bankruptcy, in poetic but also raw language." *L'Humanité*

£8.99/$13.95
Crime paperback original, ISBN 1–904738–04–4
www.bitterlemonpress.com

THE RUSSIAN PASSENGER

Günter Ohnemus

"Breathless plot in an offbeat crime novel." *Le Monde*

At fifty the good Buddhist takes to the road, leaving all his belongings behind. His sole possession is a begging bowl. That's fine. That's how it should be. The problem was, there were four million dollars in my begging bowl and the mafia were after me. It was their money. They wanted it back, and they also wanted the girl, the woman who was with me: Sonia Kovalevskaya.

So begins the story of Harry Willemer, a taxi driver and his passenger, an ex-KGB agent and wife of a Russian Mafioso. In an atmosphere of intense paranoia *The Russian Passenger* follows their flight from the hit-men sent to recover the cash. This is not only a multifaceted thriller about murder, big money and love, but also a powerful evocation of the cruel history that binds Russia and Germany.

Günter Ohnemus, born in 1946, lives in Munich and writes novels, essays and translations. He has written three collections of short stories and a best-seller for teenagers. This is his first novel to be translated into English.

"Grips you from the opening paragraphs to the very end."
Magazine Littéraire

"Simultaneously a road movie adventure, a tight thriller and an elegantly written love story." *Der Spiegel*

£9.99/$14.95
Crime paperback original, ISBN 1–904738–02–8
www.bitterlemonpress.com

HOLY SMOKE

Tonino Benacquista

"An iconoclastic chronicle of small-time crooks and desperate capers, with added Gallic and Italian flair. Wonderful fun." *The Guardian*

"This prizewinning novel is guaranteed to keep you up late at night, driven to discover the ending. It's exciting, funny and bizarrely even includes tips on cooking Italian food; it makes you glad they decided to translate the novel into English." *Coventry Evening Telegraph*

Some favours simply cannot be refused. Tonio agrees to write a love letter for Dario, a low-rent Paris gigolo. When Dario is murdered, a single bullet to the head, Tonio finds his friend has left him a small vineyard somewhere east of Naples. The wine is undrinkable but an elaborate scam has been set up. The smell of easy money attracts the unwanted attentions of the Mafia and the Vatican, and the unbridled hatred of the locals. Mafiosi aren't choir boys, and monsignors can be very much like Mafiosi. A darkly comic, iconoclastic tale told by an author of great verve and humour.

Tonino Benacquista, born in France of Italian immigrants, dropped out of film studies to finance his writing career. After being, in turn, a museum night-watchman, a train guard on the Paris-Rome line and a professional parasite on the Paris cocktail circuit, he is now a highly successful author of fiction and film scripts.

"An entertainingly cynical story. I read it in one sitting." *The Observer*

"Much to enjoy in the clash of cultures and superstitions, in a stand-off between the mafia and the Vatican. And a tasty recipe for poisoning your friends with pasta. Detail like this places European crime writing on a par with its American counterpart." *Belfast Telegraph*

£8.99
Crime paperback original, ISBN 1–904738–01–X
www.bitterlemonpress.com

GOAT SONG

Chantal Pelletier

"Tender yet ferocious, Pelletier is a lady in black to be treated with respect." *Le Canard Enchaîné*

The naked bodies of a star male dancer and a beautiful young girl have been found entwined together, murdered in a dressing room of the Moulin Rouge. A junkie is killed in a nearby flat, his throat chewed open, the teeth-marks human. Seemingly unconnected, these deaths form part of a sinister pattern involving crack dealers and addicts, wild sex parties and shady property deals.

In charge of both investigations is Maurice Laice. Depressed by what is happening to his beloved Montmartre and exhausted by the emptiness of his love life, Maurice is plagued by a female boss who bombards him with tales of her sexual exploits. Yet they make a good team, each obsessed for different reasons by the crime at hand. Together they start to uncover a twisted trail of fear and broken dreams, greed and revenge that reaches from Corsica and Algeria into the very heart of old Paris.

Chantal Pelletier, born in Lyon, began her career as a theatre actor. She founded a theatre company in Paris and is a successful author of novels, essays, plays and film scripts. She published her first *roman noir* in 1997. In *Goat Song* she introduces Maurice Laice, the world-weary inspector of three of her crime novels. *Goat Song* won the Grand Prix du roman noir of Cognac in 2001.

"Chantal Pelletier is a wonderful story teller; she captures your heart in three short sentences, and takes you through the gamut of emotions from laughter to tears. A master of funny, bittersweet dialogue. A classic roman noir hero, the world-weary inspector, is completely reinvented." *Le Monde*

£8.99
Crime paperback original, ISBN 1–904738–03–6
www.bitterlemonpress.com

IN MATTO'S REALM

Friedrich Glauser

A child murderer escapes from an insane asylum in Bern. The stakes get higher when Sergeant Studer discovers the director's body, neck broken, in the boiler room of the madhouse. Studer is drawn into the workings of an institution that darkly mirrors the world outside. Even he cannot escape the pull of the no-man's-land between reason and madness where Matto, the spirit of insanity, reigns.

This is the second in the Sergeant Studer series published by Bitter Lemon Press.

February 2005   ISBN 1–904738–06–0   £8.99/$13.95

HAVANA RED

Leonardo Padura

A young transvestite is found strangled in a Havana park. Mario Conde's investigation into a young man's violent murder exposes the equally disturbing death of his beloved Cuba.

March 2005   ISBN 1–904738–09–5   £8.99 pb

www.bitterlemonpress.com